Inspector Morimoto and the Two Umbrellas

INSPECTOR MORIMOTO AND THE TWO UMBRELLAS

A Detective Story Set in Japan

Timothy Hemion

iUniverse, Inc.
New York Lincoln Shanghai

Inspector Morimoto and the Two Umbrellas

A Detective Story Set in Japan

iUniverse, Inc.

For information address:
iUniverse, Inc.
2021 Pine Lake Road, Suite 100
Lincoln, NE 68512
www.iuniverse.com

ISBN: 0-595-30979-8 (pbk)
ISBN: 0-595-66230-7 (cloth)

Printed in the United States of America

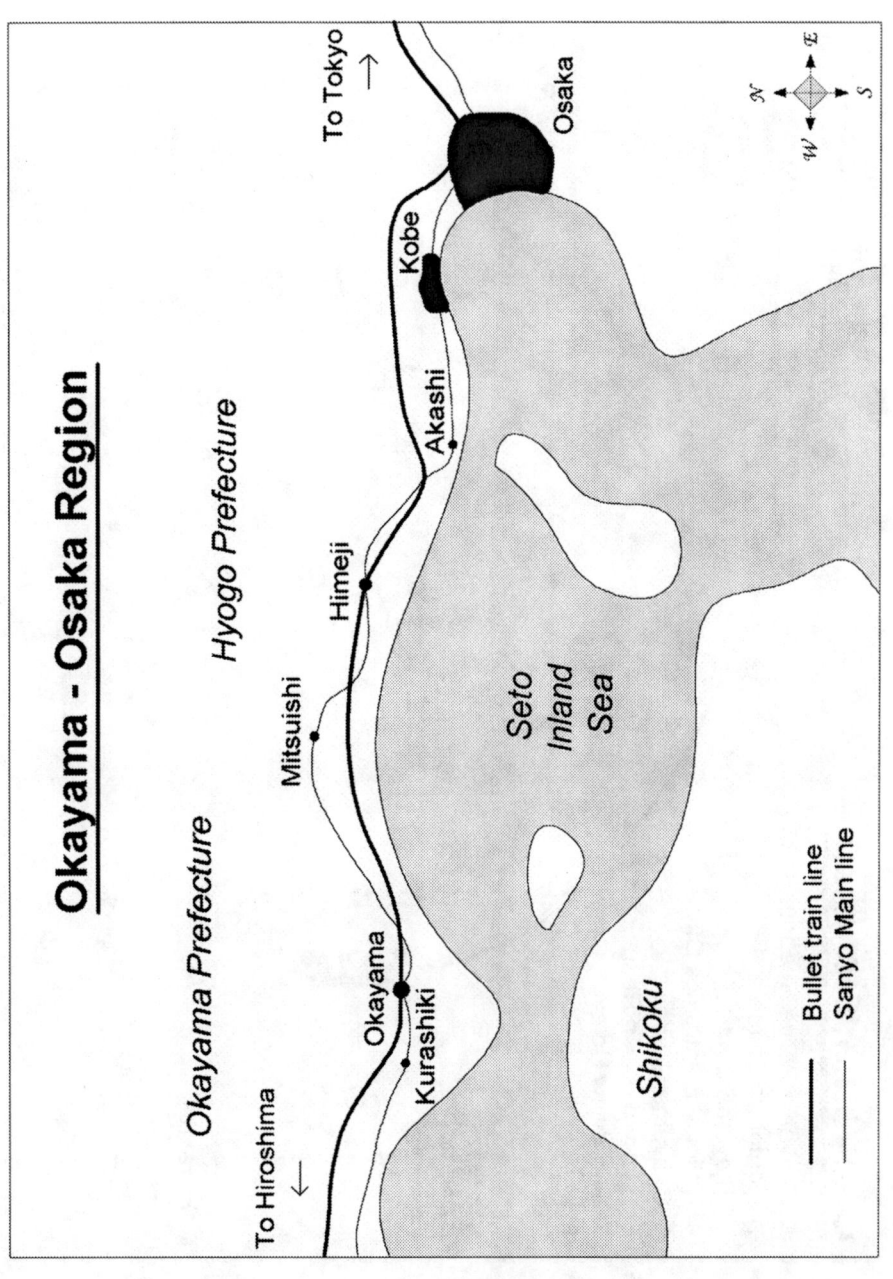

Okayama - Osaka Region

Okayama Prefecture

Hyogo Prefecture

To Hiroshima

Kurashiki

Okayama

Mitsuishi

Himeji

Akashi

Kobe

Osaka

To Tokyo

Seto Inland Sea

Shikoku

Bullet train line

Sanyo Main line

N · E · S · W

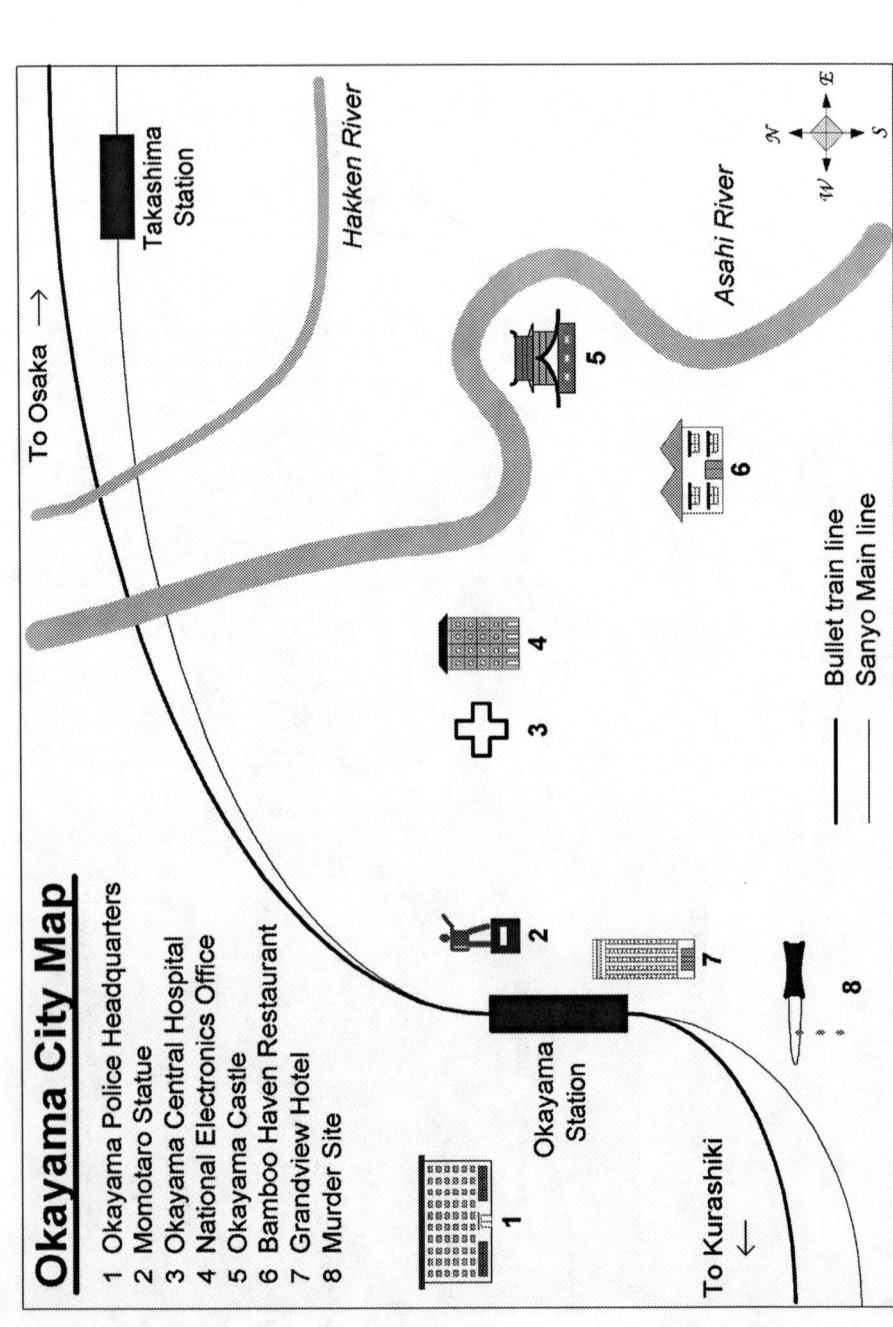

Okayama City Map

1 Okayama Police Headquarters
2 Momotaro Statue
3 Okayama Central Hospital
4 National Electronics Office
5 Okayama Castle
6 Bamboo Haven Restaurant
7 Grandview Hotel
8 Murder Site

To Osaka →

Takashima Station

Hakken River

Asahi River

Okayama Station

To Kurashiki

Bullet train line
Sanyo Main line

N W E S

CHAPTER 1

▼

Our story begins in the Japanese city of Osaka on a hot and humid Thursday evening in July. In the center of the downtown area, the brightly lit castle stood out with its white walls and green tiled roofs. Nearby a baseball game was taking place inside the Osaka Dome. On this particular evening, there was not a capacity crowd. However, it was quite a reasonable turnout—about a normal sized crowd for a midweek, midseason game hosted by the Osaka Buffaloes, a middle-of-the-table team.

Many members of the crowd, dressed in suits and ties, were businessmen who had come straight to the game from work. As they watched the game, they drank chilled beer out of plastic cups, and they ate boxed dinners of fish, meat, rice, and pickles, which they ordered from the attendants walking up and down the aisles. Holding their wooden chopsticks in one hand and their beer in the other, they chatted with their colleagues as the game progressed steadily through the early innings.

When the bottom of the fifth inning was reached, the Buffaloes had the bases loaded. Amid rising excitement and increasing clamor the Buffaloes' star hitter stepped up to the plate and took a few practice swings. He looked around at his teammates standing on their respective bases, and he stared at the coaches as they signaled instructions to him.

Throughout the stands, drummers and trumpeters were belting out a rhythmic chant, and the excited crowd clapped and shouted along in unison under the direction of their cheerleaders. The batter took the first pitch as it sailed past him into the catcher's mitt. The home plate umpire called it a strike. The batter tried out some more practice swings and took up his batting stance once again as the pitcher began his wind-up. The batter swung at the second pitch, and with a loud crack the middle of his bat made solid contact with the ball. The pitcher's head dropped in dismay as the ball sailed back over his head.

At that precise moment, a man cried out as he was being killed in Okayama city. While Osaka is the second largest city in Japan, Okayama is a much smaller city. It is located on the coast of the Seto Inland Sea about two hundred kilometers to the west of Osaka, in the opposite direction from Tokyo. Like Osaka, Okayama also has a castle that dominates the city center, although in contrast to Osaka its dark black walls and roofs provide a much more sinister appearance. While the castle gardens with their rice paddies, waterfalls, and tea plantations are considered to be among the three best classical gardens in Japan, it was a much less pleasant part of Okayama where the murder was taking place.

As the knife slashed the helpless victim in Okayama, the crowd in the Osaka Dome rose to their feet. As if in slow motion, the ball soared through the dome and over the center field wall where a fan in the twenty-second row reached up and caught it. With a big smile, she held it up for the rest of the crowd to see, and she showed it off to the television cameras that had turned to point her way. The batter tossed his bat to the ground and trotted around the bases before being congratulated by his teammates at home plate. In Okayama, the limp body slumped to the wet ground.

The Buffalo players came out from their dugout and formed a reception line for the triumphant batter, who walked along slapping the outstretched hands. When he reached the end of the line, two cheerleaders ran out and presented him with a stuffed animal. It was a buffalo with a big brown snout, a wide grin and two white horns, which was the team's mascot.

Following customary procedure, the batter hurled the stuffed animal into the crowd and stepped down into the dugout. However, he was soon called back by the crowd's prolonged cheering. He walked up to the top of the dugout steps again, stepping out to where the crowd could see him. He took off his cap and bowed several times in a circle to the rejoicing spectators.

A grand slam home run in the Osaka Dome—a lifeless body being rained upon in Okayama.

CHAPTER 2

▼

The next morning, Friday, Inspector Morimoto's bedside phone rang at five forty-five. He picked up the receiver on the second ring.

"Hello," he whispered.

"Ah, good morning, Inspector. This is Sergeant Yamada. I'm so sorry to wake you this early. It seems like there's been a murder."

Morimoto left his home fifteen minutes later, and by six thirty he was at the crime scene with Sergeant Yamada peering down at the corpse. It was raining, and Morimoto and Sergeant Yamada were both holding umbrellas to protect themselves from the downpour. The body, that of a middle-aged man in a business suit and tie, was lying in a narrow alley off a side street in a business district, about a ten minute walk to the south of the central Okayama railway station. Dawn had broken at about four thirty that morning, and not long after it had grown light the body had been discovered and the police had been alerted.

One side of the alley was formed by the tall sidewall of an office building that fronted the adjacent side street. When viewed from the alley, the building appeared slightly tatty and run down, and the rain had caused large patches of damp to show up in the concrete facade. On the other side of the alley there was a tall chain link fence behind which a yard contained a collection of old mechanical diggers and other pieces of construction equipment. Each had scuffed paintwork and clods of mud sticking to them. The tall wall along the side of the alley cut out a lot of the early morning light, and the alley was appreciably gloomier than the side street to which it was joined.

The dead man was lying on his back with a deep gash where his throat had been cut. There was a knife resting on the top of his chest with the blade pointing up towards the mutilated throat. The rain was splashing on the dead man's face and the empty eyes were wide open, staring up at the gray rain clouds.

"It looks like one of those syndicate jobs, sir," Sergeant Yamada said to Morimoto. "Look at the way they've placed the knife on his chest."

Murders in Okayama are somewhat of a novelty. However, even though Japan enjoys one of the lowest crime rates in the world, it still possesses a network of organized criminals. These syndicates operate throughout the country, and for better or worse, they have in many ways become an accepted part of Japanese life. They have many long held traditions and customs, one of which is the manner in which an assassination is carried out, if events ever reach that unsavory outcome. The murder that had aroused Morimoto from his bed, and that had taken him out into the rain early on that Friday morning, had been committed according to the syndicate tradition.

"Have the photographs been taken yet?" Morimoto asked Sergeant Yamada.

"Yes, sir."

"Good. Has anyone touched the body?"

"Not since we've been here, sir. A taxi driver called us about the body, and he said that he found it just as it is now. Other than that we don't have any other witnesses. However, we're organizing a search to see whether we can find anybody who might have seen or heard something last night or this morning."

Morimoto crouched down beside the body and peered at the knife.

"Can I have a plastic bag, please, Sergeant?"

Sergeant Yamada handed Morimoto a clear plastic bag that was used to store items of evidence, and Morimoto prodded the knife inside the bag and closed it. He handed the bag back up to Sergeant Yamada and began to search the body. In the inside pockets of the dead man's jacket, Morimoto found a wallet and a set of keys which he passed up to Sergeant Yamada as well. All the other pockets were empty, except for the outside right jacket pocket where there was a small packet of tissues, and the outside left jacket pocket where Morimoto found a short thick key attached to a bright yellow plastic tag bearing the number two hundred and three. That was all.

Morimoto stood up. He looked down at the body again and rubbed his chin as he thought for a while. He turned and looked around the alley where they were standing.

"Do you think the murder took place here, Sergeant? Or do you think that the body was just left here?"

"I don't think that we're going to be able to tell, sir, because of all the rain. If he was murdered here, then there'd have been a lot of blood on the ground, but it would all have washed away by now. I'd say that it's quite possible that the murder occurred here."

"Hmmm…yes, I agree."

Morimoto walked up and down the alley with Sergeant Yamada searching the ground.

"There don't appear to be any other clues around here, Sergeant. Incidentally, has anybody seen an umbrella?"

"An umbrella? Err…no sir. We haven't found an umbrella."

The dead man did not appear to have brought his umbrella.

"It was a nasty night to be out without an umbrella last night," Morimoto murmured.

Sergeant Yamada smiled.

"Yes, sir."

Morimoto peered down at the soaking corpse again.

"All right, you can take the body away now. I'll see you back at headquarters, Sergeant."

As the body was lifted onto a trolley and wheeled to the nearby ambulance, Morimoto slipped the key with the yellow plastic tag into his pocket. He walked at a leisurely pace by himself back down the alley to the side street, and turned towards Okayama railway station, holding his umbrella tightly against the continuing rain. Even though he did not hurry, it only took Morimoto a short time to reach the station.

Okayama railway station is a long, three-story building located almost in the center of the Okayama downtown business district. It was built to accommodate the arrival of the bullet train service that reached Okayama in 1972. The first floor of the station, on the ground level, has the ticket machines and the ticket offices, together with some travel agents and a large assortment of restaurants, shops and souvenir stands. From this floor, automatic ticket gates lead directly through to the platforms for the local railway lines, such as the Sanyo Main railway line, and escalators and stairs lead up to the second floor.

The second floor of the station provides an additional selection of restaurants, shops and souvenir stands, and there is also a further set of ticket gates that are especially for the bullet train railway lines. When the passengers for the bullet trains have passed through these ticket gates, they can then take the escalators and stairs that lead up to the third floor of the station, which is the top floor. This is where the four platforms for the bullet trains are located, and as the bullet train railway lines enter and leave the third floor of the station, they pass through Okayama city on elevated tracks.

In the pedestrian concourse outside Okayama station, next to the bus stops and the taxi ranks, there is a large bronze statue of Momotaro, the boy hero of one of the most beloved of all Japanese folktales. The statue is set high up on a marble plinth overlooking a water fountain, surrounded by a series of small flowerbeds. In the statue, Momotaro is depicted as a young man dressed in traditional Japanese garments and shoes. He is marching forward, and his left hand is raised to shield his eyes as he looks out into the distance. His right hand is down by his side carrying a fan, and he also has a sword strapped around his waist. His companions in the folktale are a pheasant, a dog, and a monkey, and these are also shown in the statue. Momotaro's statue is a popular meeting place for children, and even adults, as we shall learn later on in our story.

As he entered the station lobby, Morimoto closed his umbrella and walked over to a newsstand where he bought a copy of the Okayama Tribune, the main Okayama morning newspaper. He glanced at the headlines as he rode the escalator up to the second floor and entered one of the restaurants. He ordered a breakfast of rice, grilled fish, and fermented soybean soup with tofu and seaweed. As he ate his meal, he read through the main news stories and most of the sports pages featuring the previous evening's baseball results, particularly the game in the Osaka Dome and the Buffaloes' fifth inning grand slam home run. Morimoto finished his meal with a cup of black coffee.

When he had finished his breakfast, Morimoto left the restaurant and took an escalator back down to the first floor lobby. The morning rush hour was just getting underway, and he walked through the crowd of commuters to one of the tram stops on the main road passing by the station. He boarded a waiting tram, and sat for a few moments looking out of the window before the doors closed and it departed. Morimoto stepped off the tram at the third stop, crossed over to the side of the road, and walked up the steps of the police headquarters. Inside he took the elevator to the fourth floor, and walked along the corridor towards his office that was shared by his assistant, Police Officer Suzuki.

"Good morning, sir," Suzuki said as Morimoto entered the office and placed his wet umbrella in the stand.

"Ah, good morning, Suzuki. It seems like we've another syndicate killing on our hands."

"Yes, Sergeant Yamada has been telling me about it, sir. If the previous cases of syndicate assassinations are anything to go by, it's not likely that we'll be able to make much progress on it, I suppose."

"Hmmm…that may well be true. Oh, one thing though. The dead man had this in his pocket."

Morimoto walked over to Suzuki's desk and showed her the key that he had found in the dead man's jacket. It was a key that belonged to a kind of public coin locker that can be found throughout Japan, particularly at railway stations such as Okayama station, and other similar public places. It had a series of small numbers engraved into the top edge that provided information on the locker to which it belonged.

"Could you find out where it's from, please?" Morimoto asked.

Suzuki wrote down the number from the key and gave it back to Morimoto who walked back to his desk and sat down. Suzuki typed away on her computer.

"Just a moment, sir," she said, "it shouldn't take long. Let me see…ah, yes, here it is. It didn't come from very far away, sir, as might have been expected. It's from Kurashiki railway station."

"Oh, I see. Thank you."

Kurashiki is a city close by Okayama, and in fact the two cities are now practically joined together by their recent urban expansions.

Morimoto sat back in his chair and wondered what he should do next. He picked up the phone and was about to call Sergeant Yamada to ask him if he would make a trip to Kurashiki to see what was in the station coin locker, but he changed his mind before dialing and replaced the receiver. Instead, he rose from his desk and retrieved his umbrella from the stand in the corner of the office.

"Suzuki, would you please take a look at the wallet we found this morning. Sergeant Yamada has it. There was also a bunch of keys. Oh, and Sergeant Yamada has the knife as well."

"Very well, sir."

"I'm going to Kurashiki to check the locker. I don't expect that I'll be too long."

Morimoto left the room and headed back towards the elevators, umbrella in hand. Upon leaving the police headquarters, he returned to Okayama station by tram, and he purchased a ticket to Kurashiki from one of the automatic ticket machines on the walls of the station lobby. He used his ticket to pass through the automatic ticket gate to the platforms, and he boarded the train waiting at the platform directly in front of him. It was heading westward on the Sanyo Main railway line.

Five minutes later, when the train had filled to about half capacity, there was a short warning siren and the doors of the carriages banged shut. The train pulled slowly out of the station and passed through the business district very close to the alley where the murder victim had been found that morning. Soon, however, the scenery changed to the more pleasant greenery of the Japanese countryside, and

Morimoto enjoyed the views of the farmhouses and the rice fields. At the second stop, Morimoto looked out at the new baseball stadium, named Muscat Stadium in recognition of the local grape cultivation.

Fourteen minutes and three stops after leaving Okayama station, Morimoto stepped off the train at Kurashiki station. He climbed the stairs from the platform and surrendered his ticket at the automatic ticket gate. To his left there were several rows of taxis waiting to take tourists to the famous Edo period buildings and warehouses of the local samurai, but Morimoto turned right, heading instead in the direction of the modern Tivoli garden amusement park, styled after the original Tivoli gardens in Copenhagen.

The coin lockers were located in a small vestibule off to the right from the main station concourse, and Morimoto surveyed the rows of lockers. Most of the lockers had a key in the door, attached to a bright yellow plastic tag displaying the locker number. This number was also written on the locker door. These were the unused, unlocked lockers, and their doors could be opened and belongings could be placed inside. However, the keys could not be turned or removed from the lockers until three hundred yen had been deposited in the adjoining money slot. Once the required money had been inserted, the key could be turned and removed. The locker was then locked. Just as Morimoto had expected, locker two hundred and three did not have a key in it.

There were two sizes of lockers. Most of the lockers were of the smaller kind with the door being roughly square-shaped. This size was suitable for storing a handbag, a briefcase or a small backpack. On the other hand, the bottom rows of lockers were substantially larger, being much taller than they were wide, so that they might accommodate a typical sized suitcase, for example. Locker two hundred and three was one of the larger kinds. Morimoto removed the key from his pocket and crouched down besides the locker. The key slid smoothly into the keyhole. Suzuki had found the right set of lockers.

During the train ride from Okayama, Morimoto had been wondering what he was likely to find inside the locker. After spending over twenty-five years in the police force working in Okayama, it had become quite unusual for Morimoto to be very much surprised by anything that he encountered while performing his duties. He had become quite accustomed to human habits and behavior patterns, while at the same time he also had observed sufficient examples of human eccentricity and outlandish conduct that he was rarely put in the position of having to raise an eyebrow in astonishment.

Over the years he had settled comfortably into the life of a detective. His colleagues wondered whether he was disappointed at having been passed over for the more glamorous postings, the transfers to the big cities, the prestige and the recognition. Actually, his promotion to inspector had been well overdue when it had finally arrived. "He's too old fashioned," his colleagues whispered amongst themselves.

Morimoto was of an average height for a Japanese male, and he also had an average build. He was clean-shaven, with quite short straight black hair, and he wore circular gold-rimmed spectacles. He had a dark, suntanned face, which many people judged to betray a certain degree of kindness in his personality. During the hot summer months, Morimoto tended to favor very lightweight suits, and on this day he was wearing a light gray suit with a white shirt and a straightforward striped tie. He was also wearing comfortable black shoes, and on his left wrist he wore a silver wristwatch.

Morimoto turned the key and opened the locker door.

"Hmmm…that's very interesting," he murmured to himself.

On this rainy, Friday morning in July, Morimoto was surprised by what he found inside locker two hundred and three. In fact, it was probably the only thing that would have surprised him. The locker was completely empty.

CHAPTER 3

▼

Police Officer Suzuki was waiting for Inspector Morimoto when he returned to the office.

"I've been through the wallet, sir, and I've also made some inquiries. The dead man is a Mr. Atsushi Sekikawa, a forty-three-year-old businessman. He lived in an apartment in Kurashiki, although his wife and young son apparently moved to Tokyo about five years ago. He was employed by National Electronics, one of the large computer companies here in Okayama. He worked in their head office the other side of Okayama station, next to the Okayama Central Hospital."

"Has his wife been notified yet?" Morimoto asked.

"Yes, sir, I was able to get in touch with her myself."

"Well done. When was the last time that she saw her husband? Did you ask her?"

"Yes, I did, sir. She told me that she hadn't seen her husband since they separated five years ago."

"Oh, I see."

Morimoto thought for a moment.

"Were you able to find out anything about why she moved to Tokyo?"

"I did try to probe a little," Suzuki replied. "She said that their relationship had developed difficulties, and she seemed to indicate that the cause had been money problems, although she didn't elaborate."

"Hmmm...I see."

Morimoto sat down at his desk.

"How upset was she about the news of her husband's death? Were you able to tell?"

"Actually, she didn't appear particularly emotional at all upon hearing the news, sir. Perhaps just a little shocked, as might be expected."

"Yes, of course."

Morimoto leaned back in his chair and watched the raindrops run down the window. Suzuki looked over from her desk.

"And also, sir, I was able to get in touch with Mr. Sekikawa's landlady. I told her that we'd be sending somebody over there today to take a look at his apartment."

Morimoto nodded.

"Yes, good. I think that we should go ourselves, later this morning."

"Very well, sir. And I've been in touch with National Electronics."

"Oh, really? What did you learn from them?"

"Well, first of all they agreed to have one of their employees go over to the morgue to identify the body. They said that they'd send one of Mr. Sekikawa's colleagues."

"Good idea. Did you find out if he was at work yesterday?"

"Yes, he was, sir. They said that he was there all day yesterday, in the head office."

"And when did he leave? Do they know at what time he left his office yesterday?"

"I asked them, of course, and they said that they think he must have left at about six fifteen yesterday evening."

"I see. That all sounds quite normal, doesn't it?"

"Yes, sir. I was also able to find out that the head of Mr. Sekikawa's division is a Mr. Ishihara, but I was told that he's away on a business trip in Osaka. He's been notified of Mr. Sekikawa's death and he's returning to Okayama this afternoon. I've told the company that we'll need to speak with him when he gets back."

"Yes, thank you."

There was a sharp knock on the door and Sergeant Yamada strode into the office.

"The body's been identified, sir," he said to Morimoto. "His office sent somebody over to the morgue. It's Mr. Sekikawa all right."

"Thank you, Sergeant."

"And I've brought you the initial medical report, sir, from Dr. Ogata."

Sergeant Yamada handed Morimoto a folder.

"Thank you. Oh, Sergeant, could you please have one of our technicians go over to Kurashiki station and take a look at a coin locker—number two hundred and three—it's one of the large lockers. I'd like to know whether there's any evidence that the locker has been broken into, or if the lock has been picked, for example."

"Very well, sir."

"And another thing, Sergeant. We're going to need to know what the syndicates have to say about this. Perhaps you could get in touch with Mrs. Tanaka? She might have something useful to tell us."

"I'll go and see her myself, sir."

Mrs. Tanaka owned a bar that was popular with syndicate members and other elements of the criminal community, among whom she had many friends and contacts. When the occasion arose, she was not averse to sharing information with the police and providing an insight into the syndicates' activities.

After Sergeant Yamada had left, Morimoto got up from his desk and poured two cups of green tea from the teapot on the desk in the middle of the office, one for himself and one for Suzuki. He took Suzuki's tea over to her, and then he sat down at his desk again and read through the medical report.

"There's not much new here, Suzuki," Morimoto said as he closed the report and placed it on his desk. "It's all pretty much as expected. Dr. Ogata confirms that the death was as a result of the victim having his throat cut. She says that there wasn't any evidence of a struggle, and that the killing was done very quickly and expertly. The implication is that the assassin knew what he or she was doing."

"That fits in with the other indications that it was a syndicate assassination, sir."

"Yes, exactly. The report says that Mr. Sekikawa's throat was cut by somebody who was standing behind him. Therefore, it would seem that he was taken by surprise and that would account for the lack of a struggle. It also says, that his throat was slashed by a right-handed assailant using a very sharp knife. Well, that certainly fits in with the knife that we found. What did you make of that knife, Suzuki?"

"It's just an ordinary kitchen knife, sir, very sharp, but not at all difficult to get a hold of. They're sold all over the place. It's certainly sharp enough to have cut Mr. Sekikawa's throat. I've sent it off for a finger print analysis and to have the blade examined."

"Good. If it was a syndicate killing though, there's not likely to be any fingerprints on the knife—they're far too careful for that. Anyway, there is one interesting point in the medical report. Dr. Ogata has estimated the time of death as being somewhere between seven o'clock and nine o'clock last night."

"Ah, well that would fit in with Mr. Sekikawa leaving his office at six fifteen."

"Yes," Morimoto agreed. "I wonder, though, whether the killing was done before it became dark, or after?"

"Well, it started getting dark at about seven o'clock, sir, but it wasn't completely dark until around eight o'clock. If Mr. Sekikawa was murdered in the alley where his body was found this morning, then it seems likely that the murderer would have waited until after eight o'clock. If the murder took place in the alley between eight o'clock and nine o'clock, then the body could easily have remained unnoticed until the taxi driver saw it this morning."

"Yes, that would make sense. There isn't any lighting in the alley at nighttime, and it's quite possible that there wouldn't have been any traffic either."

Morimoto leaned back in his chair and rested his legs up on the corner of his desk. He removed his spectacles and he rubbed his eyes and face. Replacing his spectacles, he locked his hands behind his neck and closed his eyes. He sat and pondered over the morning's events.

After a few moments, he looked over at Suzuki again who was working on her computer.

"You know, Suzuki, there wasn't anything in the coin locker."

Suzuki looked a little surprised. She stopped what she was doing and leaned on her desk, resting her chin in her hand as she looked back at Morimoto.

"Nothing at all, sir?"

"Nothing," Morimoto confirmed.

"That's interesting," Suzuki said, after a pause.

Morimoto gazed thoughtfully out of the window.

"Yes, rather a waste of three hundred yen, I'd say."

Towards the end of the morning, Morimoto set off for Kurashiki to take a look around Mr. Sekikawa's apartment. It was his second trip to Kurashiki that day, and this time he took Suzuki with him. Suzuki had been working with Morimoto since April of the previous year when she had graduated with honors from the prestigious Tokyo University with a degree in mathematics. Not many students join the police force after finishing a mathematics degree, but the disciplines of mathematics and crime detection do in fact have many very basic similarities. The ability to exploit patterns and to identify inconsistencies is a fundamental necessity for any good mathematician, and also for any good police detective, as Suzuki had often tried to explain to her friends.

Suzuki was the kind of person with whom Morimoto enjoyed working. She was meticulous, thorough, and she thought problems through in a logical manner. And above all else, she had a sharp mind and an inquisitive nature. In these respects, she was rather like Morimoto. As their partnership had developed over the year in which they had worked together, they had both acquired an understanding and respect for each other's abilities.

Morimoto and Suzuki traveled to Kurashiki by train on the Sanyo Main line, just as Morimoto had done earlier that day. It was still raining, although that was not unusual since the annual rainy season in Okayama generally lasts from the end of June until almost the end of July. During the rainy season it rains most days and nights, and the rain is accompanied by incessant high temperatures and high humidity, so that weather wise it is a trying time for the Okayama inhabitants.

Instead of using a taxi at Kurashiki station, Morimoto and Suzuki decided to take a bus to Mr. Sekikawa's apartment. The bus that they needed was waiting in the rows of bus stops adjacent to the station, and it left after only a few minutes. Ten minutes later, Morimoto and Suzuki stepped off the bus about a block away from the eight-story apartment building that was their destination, and they sheltered under their umbrellas as they walked down the street. The apartment building had a brick facade and looked to be well maintained, and Morimoto judged it to be slightly more classy than the average level of apartments in Kurashiki, although definitely not at the top of the range.

Morimoto and Suzuki shook their umbrellas dry on the steps of the apartment building and went inside. They introduced themselves to the landlady who was waiting for them in the first floor lobby outside her office, and they showed her their police identification cards.

"Thank you for taking the time to meet us," Morimoto said.

"Oh, it's quite all right, Inspector," the landlady replied. "It's no trouble at all. Of course, we're all very shocked here at the terrible news. I've been discussing it with some of the other tenants."

Morimoto could see a small group of people in the landlady's office, and he was not surprised to see that their ostensibly shocked demeanors also revealed a slight touch of excitement as they digested the news of the demise of one of their fellow residents.

"We can't believe it," the landlady continued. "He seemed such a nice man, Mr. Sekikawa—very quiet, and he always minded his own business. We never had any trouble from him."

"We'd like to look through his apartment, please," Morimoto asked.

"Yes, of course, Inspector. It's on the third floor. We can go up in the elevator. I'll show you where it is. I have the key with me."

The three of them rode up to the third floor in the small elevator and the landlady led them along the corridor and unlocked one of the doors.

"I'll wait for you downstairs," she said, "unless you need me here?"

Morimoto shook his head.

"No, no, we can manage, I think. Thank you."

The landlady walked back towards the elevator.

Morimoto and Suzuki entered the apartment and looked around. It was a rather small one-bedroom apartment that appeared to be fairly tidy, clean, and well looked after. It was quite comfortably furnished, although not at all luxuriously. Working silently, Morimoto and Suzuki began a systematic and thorough search through the contents. Rummaging through a dead man's belongings, especially those of somebody who had died so recently, was not particularly enjoyable for either of them. "I suppose that being murdered does impose certain demands on one's privacy," Morimoto thought to himself.

It took about thirty minutes for Morimoto and Suzuki to complete their examination, and they were both glad when they had finished.

"Well, Suzuki, I haven't noticed anything unusual here, have you?" Morimoto asked.

"No, sir. There doesn't appear to be anything out of the ordinary."

"However, there's obviously been a lady using the apartment as well—a girl-friend, probably. What do you think?"

"Yes. I had a look in the wardrobe, and whoever she is she keeps quite a few of her clothes here, so I'd imagine that she's a fairly regular visitor. Maybe the land-lady will be able to tell us something about her."

"Hmmm…let's go and ask her."

Morimoto and Suzuki closed the apartment door behind them and took the elevator back down to the first floor where the landlady came out from her office again to meet them.

"Is everything all right, Inspector?" the landlady asked, without being able to completely hide her curiosity. "Did you find anything important?"

"Oh, everything's fine, thank you," Morimoto replied. "By the way, how long has Mr. Sekikawa been living here?"

"A little over two years now. He's one of our newest tenants. Some of our residents have been here for over ten years. Mr. Sekikawa renewed his lease just last month, as a matter of fact."

"And that would be for another year, would it? Did he renew his lease for a full year?"

"Yes, that's right. We only have yearly leases here."

"What kind of a resident was he?"

"Oh, as I said, we've never had any trouble from him. He was always very quiet. I didn't see him very often."

"Do you know who stayed with him? Was it his girlfriend?"

"He did have a girlfriend, yes. She stayed here now and again, I think. But I don't know who she was. I never really met her."

"I see."

Morimoto thought for a moment and rubbed his chin.

"When was the last time that you saw Mr. Sekikawa?"

"Let me see...I saw him last weekend. It was on Sunday afternoon. I saw him as he was leaving the building. I haven't seen him since then."

"So you didn't see him yesterday evening, then?"

"No, no. I'm sure that I haven't seen him since last Sunday."

"Do you know, perhaps, whether Mr. Sekikawa returned to his apartment last night?"

The landlady shrugged.

"I don't know, sorry. He might have been here, or he might not. I really don't know one way or the other."

Morimoto thanked the landlady again, and as he walked out of the building with Suzuki, he noticed that the group of people crowded into the landlady's office had grown appreciably in number, and that they were showing significantly less shock, and perceptibly more excitement.

As they rode back to Okayama on the train, Morimoto went over in his mind the various things that he had learned that day. The empty coin locker in Kurashiki particularly intrigued him. In addition to that, he wondered how important it was that he had not been able to find something in Mr. Sekikawa's apartment—something that he had particularly been looking for. He turned to Suzuki who was sitting beside him next to the window.

"You know, Suzuki, there wasn't an umbrella in Mr. Sekikawa's apartment."

Suzuki nodded.

"Yes, that's right, sir. There wasn't an umbrella. I also noticed that."

The train rattled its way into Okayama and passed close by the murder scene where Morimoto had stood in the rain at six thirty that morning, looking down at Mr. Sekikawa's soaking body.

"And you also mentioned, sir, that there wasn't an umbrella in the alley where Mr. Sekikawa was found this morning, isn't that right?"

"Yes, quite right, Suzuki. Quite right."

"Well, I wonder where Mr. Sekikawa's umbrella is, then?" Suzuki pondered as the train pulled into Okayama station.

"That's a very good question, Suzuki."

CHAPTER 4

▼

It was early afternoon when Inspector Morimoto and Police Officer Suzuki returned to their office at police headquarters. Sergeant Yamada was waiting for them.

"I was able to arrange a meeting with Mrs. Tanaka, sir," Sergeant Yamada reported. "She says that the news about last night's killing has spread quickly among the syndicates, but they're all insisting that they weren't involved. From what she's heard, the syndicates don't know anything about the murder last night. At least, none of them are admitting that they know anything. But they do know Mr. Sekikawa, sir. He's been quite involved with the syndicates, it seems."

"Oh, really?" Morimoto said as he sat down at his desk. "In what way?"

"Mrs. Tanaka said that it was all about money, sir. He owed them a lot of money. From what Mrs. Tanaka was able to gather, Mr. Sekikawa had been losing money at the gambling clubs run by the syndicates for a number of years, and apparently he'd taken out loans to cover his gambling debts. And then he'd also gambled and lost some of the money that he'd borrowed. He was in very deep trouble, sir. The syndicates are very touchy about people who owe them money."

"Well then, Sergeant, it would appear that Mr. Sekikawa was well known to the criminal community."

"Exactly, sir."

"By the way, Sergeant, we're going to have to find Mr. Sekikawa's girlfriend. Perhaps you could ask at his office? One of his colleagues must know who she is."

"I'll get on to that right away, sir," Sergeant Yamada replied, and left the office.

Later that afternoon there was a sharp knock on the door and Sergeant Yamada returned.

"Mr. Ishihara has arrived, sir—Mr. Sekikawa's boss at National Electronics. He came back from Osaka on the Nozomi bullet train this afternoon and we sent a car to pick him up at the station. He's waiting for you in one of the second floor interview rooms."

The Nozomi is the fastest of the bullet trains that run from Tokyo to Osaka, and then pass through Okayama on their way to Hiroshima and further west. The Nozomi bullet train covers the one hundred and thirteen miles between Shin-Osaka station in Osaka and Okayama station in exactly forty-two minutes.

Morimoto took the elevator down to the second floor and walked along the corridor to the interview room where Mr. Ishihara was waiting. He knocked on the door, and Mr. Ishihara stood up as he entered. They bowed politely to each other—formal bows with the upper part of the body inclined a full thirty degrees from the vertical. At this, their first meeting, and in police headquarters on the occasion of a murder, it would have been quite impolite to bow any less formally.

Morimoto and Mr. Ishihara sat down in comfortable chairs on either side of a well-polished, rectangular wooden table in the middle of the room. The window-less interview room was carpeted, but it had no furnishings other than the table and some chairs. A lady knocked gently on the door and entered the room. She served them both hot green tea in small round cups sitting on wooden saucers, and then she bowed and left the room, closing the door quietly behind her.

Morimoto looked over at Mr. Ishihara, who appeared to be in his late fifties. He was below average height, and heavily built with thinning black hair and a narrow moustache. He looked apprehensive and tired, and he was perspiring slightly. He was dressed in an expensive businessman's dark suit and tie, and his large briefcase was on the floor next to his chair. He had also brought a dark red umbrella with him that he had propped up against the table.

Mr. Ishihara took his handkerchief out from his pocket and wiped his forehead several times.

"Thank you for coming here," Morimoto began. "I hope that it's not been too inconvenient for you? It's just routine in matters of this kind that we ask you a few questions."

"Yes, of course, Inspector. I quite understand. This has come as a great shock to me. I've known Mr. Sekikawa since he joined National Electronics more than ten years ago. In fact, he's been working in my division for more than five years now. When I was telephoned this morning in Osaka and told about it—his death

I mean—I really couldn't believe it! They told me that he'd been found dead lying in a street somewhere. They said that he'd been murdered. Is that correct? Can you tell me exactly what happened? Have you caught the people who did it?"

Morimoto explained how a taxi driver had discovered Mr. Sekikawa's body that morning, and that he had been found with his throat cut.

Mr. Ishihara adjusted his tie and wiped his neck with his handkerchief.

"It's all so inconceivable!"

Morimoto nodded and sipped his tea.

"Has Mr. Sekikawa been having any problems at work recently? Or has there perhaps been anything unusual about his conduct?"

Mr. Ishihara shrugged.

"No, no problems at all. His work has been going very well, and he hasn't been acting any differently from usual. At least, I haven't been aware of anything. Everything has been quite normal. We've all been very busy this year, of course, and so we've all been under a lot of stress. We've been involved in a very important project. My division's been working on it full-time. Nevertheless, I can't say that there's been anything unusual about Mr. Sekikawa. Nothing at all—nothing that I've noticed in any case."

Morimoto paused and thought for a moment before continuing.

"Were you aware that Mr. Sekikawa had any money problems?"

Mr. Ishihara appeared embarrassed. He picked up his teacup in his right hand and swallowed a few mouthfuls of tea.

"Well, yes. We all pretty much knew about that, all of us in the division. It's not something that you can keep a secret, really. But I never discussed the matter with him personally. I didn't like to go into his private matters. That's a rule I try to keep with all of the people in my division. Nevertheless, as I said, a lot of us knew about his money problems. It's the kind of topic that attracts gossip. He'd taken out several loans, I believe, and he'd had difficulties with the payments. That's what I heard anyway. I think that gambling caused his problems. At least, I think that's how it all started. A great shame really. But he was a good worker, Mr. Sekikawa. I can vouch for that. His personal problems didn't seem to get in the way of his work."

"Did you ever meet his wife?"

"His wife?"

Mr. Ishihara wiped his forehead again and considered the question for a moment.

"Well she left him, you know. She went off somewhere, didn't she? Didn't she move to Tokyo? That was quite a few years ago. I think that I might have met her before she left him. Perhaps just after Mr. Sekikawa joined the company, but I'm not certain."

Morimoto nodded.

"So, you haven't met his wife recently, then?"

"Oh, no, certainly not recently."

"Do you know whether he had any other relationships then? A girlfriend perhaps?"

Mr. Ishihara shook his head.

"I wouldn't know anything about that. He may well have had a girlfriend. Some of the other people in the division ought to know. Probably some of his colleagues could tell you."

Morimoto sipped his tea and there were a few more moments of silence. Then he looked up at Mr. Ishihara again.

"Well, I'm sorry to have had to take up so much of your time. I'm sure that you must be very busy. As I said, I hope that this hasn't been too much of an inconvenience for you. By the way, you said that you've been in Osaka, didn't you?"

"Yes, that's right. I've just come back from Osaka this afternoon."

"How long were you in Osaka?"

"Just a few days. I left Okayama the day before yesterday, Wednesday. I took the morning Nozomi bullet train."

"I see. What were you doing in Osaka?"

"Oh, visiting one of our contractors, Consolidated Chipboards. They're important partners of ours. I visit them quite regularly, as a matter of fact."

"How often is that?"

"Oh, maybe once or twice a month, I imagine, on average."

"Do you always stay overnight in Osaka on these trips?"

"Oh, yes. Whenever I go there I generally have business on more than one day, so I naturally stay there one or two nights."

Morimoto swirled the last drops of tea around in the bottom of his teacup.

"What were you doing last night, Mr. Ishihara?"

"Last night? Me?"

Mr. Ishihara seemed surprised and he laughed a little nervously.

"Well, I went to a baseball game, actually. My meetings didn't drag on very late yesterday. I was finished by late afternoon, so I was able to get to the Osaka Dome for the start of the game. You know, to watch the Osaka Buffaloes. I like to watch a game whenever I can. Unfortunately, that's not nearly as often as I wish. It was a very good game last night, though. Did you hear about it? It was really very exciting."

Mr. Ishihara smiled and wiped his forehead again. Morimoto put down his teacup.

"Well thank you for helping me, Mr. Ishihara, and as I said, I'm very sorry for the inconvenience. I'll order a police car for you. Where would you like to go? To your office?"

"Yes, thank you. A ride to my office would be very helpful."

Mr. Ishihara collected his briefcase and his umbrella, and Morimoto took him down to the first floor and arranged a police car for him. As they parted company, Morimoto expressed his condolences over Mr. Sekikawa, and they bowed to each other once again.

Morimoto returned to his office on the fourth floor at the end of what had turned out to be a long day. He felt tired. Suzuki was out somewhere, and Morimoto wondered what else he could usefully do that afternoon. He had just decided to get up and go home when Sergeant Yamada appeared again.

"You're wanted upstairs, sir, by the Chief. His secretary just called."

Morimoto took the elevator up to the seventh floor and was ushered into the Chief's office by his secretary. The Chief of Police was in his middle sixties with thin gray hair and a bulging waistline. He had been in charge of the Okayama Police Department for almost ten years, and he oversaw its activities almost like a father figure, with great pride and affection. His large face was always quick to show his feelings, especially his irritation if he ever became aware of any ineffi-ciency within his police force, but he was also equally quick to recognize and praise good police work whenever he saw it.

"Ah, good afternoon, Morimoto," the Chief said as Morimoto walked into the office. "I'm glad that you could come up. Do sit down. And let me introduce you to Mr. Nishi. He's from Tokyo—works in the Special Branch office."

Morimoto nodded at Mr. Nishi, who appeared to be slightly younger than Morimoto. He was tall with a slight build and a thin narrow face. The Special Branch office in Tokyo handled important cases of national interest, and became involved in a wide range of activities from ordinary police matters to interna-tional espionage. In Morimoto's opinion, they tended to be very secretive and were inclined to look down on the rest of the police force. Morimoto did not expect that Mr. Nishi would be very impressed by a provincial inspector such as himself.

"We're interested in the murder case that you've been working on today," the Chief continued. "A Mr. Atsushi Sekikawa, I believe. Terrible thing, isn't it? We'd like to know what you've found out about it. How's it going? Have you been able to make much progress?"

Morimoto reflected for a moment before answering.

"Well, sir," he said slowly, "it would at first sight appear to be a straightforward syndicate killing. Mr. Sekikawa was assassinated in the distinctive syndicate fashion, as I'm sure that you've heard. And at the moment, there's nothing definite to suggest that there's anything more to it than that. And as for the motive, well it seems that he was up to his neck in debt to the syndicates. He had been for a number of years, apparently."

Morimoto paused before continuing.

"Well, this kind of thing has happened before, sir. Usually, it's not a very good return on an investment to kill somebody who owes you money. Rather a bad business policy you might say. Most of the time, in these circumstances the syndicates will do no more than threaten, and they can of course make life very difficult for you. But once in a while they decide to make an example, I suppose. It frightens the other people who owe them money, I imagine."

"Yes, exactly Morimoto," the Chief said. "Mr. Nishi and myself, we imagined that it must be something like that."

There were a few moments of silence. Morimoto was wondering what Mr. Nishi had to do with Mr. Sekikawa's murder, and he was also deliberating whether or not he should tell the Chief about the key to the empty coin locker at Kurashiki station. Before he had made up his mind, the Chief spoke up again.

"Do you think that you'll be able to find the murderer, Morimoto?"

"Well, sir, as you know these syndicate murders are rarely solved. Judging from what we know so far, I don't think that we'll be able to pin this on anybody. Not unless any witnesses come forward, that is. We've been searching for people who might have been in that area last night—who might have seen something. But we haven't had any luck so far."

There was silence again in the Chief's office. Then the Chief glanced over at Mr. Nishi, who nodded slightly. With this sign of assent, the Chief started out again, this time talking much more slowly than before.

"Morimoto, there's something that you might need to know about this case. It's about the company where Mr. Sekikawa worked, National Electronics. Well, to get straight to the point, it's been under investigation for the past six months or so. Tokyo is running it. Mr. Nishi here is in charge. That's why he's here today. It's very hush-hush, undercover work. I'm sure that you know the kind of thing. The fact is that this company has been doing some rather sensitive research work, you see. Work of real national importance, actually. I'm afraid that I can't tell you the details of the research. I'm sure that you'll understand. A lot of the work is done in Mr. Sekikawa's division, the division headed by Mr. Ishihara. I believe that you met him this afternoon? Anyway, the point is that there've been some alleged leaks—overseas, as a matter of fact. A very severe case of industrial espionage."

The Chief frowned, as if to emphasize the seriousness of what he was explaining.

"It's a very grave business," he continued, "as I'm sure you'll appreciate. I can't really tell you much more about it now. Anyway, I thought that you'd better know about the Tokyo investigation, although I don't expect that it's going to interfere with your work. We'll be very interested if anything unusual does turn up in Mr. Sekikawa's murder case, of course. And we'll be keeping a close eye on how you get on, as a matter of fact, won't we Mr. Nishi?"

Mr. Nishi nodded.

"And Morimoto," the Chief added, "I don't mind telling you that it's a pleasure to cooperate with Mr. Nishi and Special Branch. They do such top quality police work. They're at the peak of the profession, I'll say! And I have to admit that I'm learning a thing or two as well. When this is all over, we'll have to see about implementing some of their techniques right here in the Okayama Police Department!"

The Chief smiled at Mr. Nishi who showed no reaction to the compliments.

The Chief's homage to Special Branch seemed to be an indication that the meeting was over, but Morimoto waited for a moment.

"Excuse me, sir," Morimoto said. "If that's the case—leaks from National Electronics—then doesn't that mean that, potentially at least, somebody from Mr. Ishihara's division could be connected with Mr. Sekikawa's murder? It certainly raises the possibility that somebody from the division might have had a motive for the murder, don't you think?"

Mr. Nishi shifted uncomfortably in his chair.

"Yes, well, Morimoto," the Chief replied, "if that's the case then I'm sure that Mr. Nishi and his team will get to the bottom of the matter in no time at all."

Morimoto rode the elevator back down to the fourth floor. He was feeling even more tired now than before his meeting with the Chief, and he was ready to go home. When he stopped by his office to pick up his umbrella and briefcase, he saw that Suzuki had returned.

"Here's something for you to think about tonight, Suzuki. Why would anybody be walking around carrying a key to a coin locker that's empty?"

Suzuki nodded.

"Yes, exactly, sir. That's a very interesting question. I wonder why?"

In fact, Morimoto and Suzuki both spent their Friday evening considering that question very carefully indeed.

CHAPTER 5

▼

The next morning, Saturday, was hot and humid and it was still raining. When Inspector Morimoto arrived at his office, Police Officer Suzuki was already at her desk typing away at her computer.

"Have there been any new developments?" Morimoto asked.

"Well, sir, we've received a report on the knife, the murder weapon. As expected, there weren't any fingerprints on it. It yielded no clues at all, unfortunately, but it was confirmed as having been the knife that cut Mr. Sekikawa's throat."

"I see."

"Mr. Sekikawa's keys have been checked as well, sir. Again, there's nothing unusual about them. They're simply his apartment and office keys. And Sergeant Yamada told me that we're still looking for witnesses who may have seen something at the alley, but that nothing has come up yet. Oh, and the report on the Kurashiki coin locker has also come in, sir."

"Good. What does it tell us?"

"Basically, there's no sign of anything abnormal about the locker, sir. Our technicians have been over it very carefully, and they say that there's no evidence that the locker has been broken into forcibly, or that the lock has been picked. I also called the station officials and asked them whether they knew of anything unusual that had happened with the locker. They said that didn't know of anything."

Morimoto sat down at his desk. He tilted his chair backwards, locked his hands behind his neck and put his feet up on the desk. It was his favorite thinking position. After a few moments, he looked over at Suzuki.

"What are your ideas about this locker, then, Suzuki? Why do you think that Mr. Sekikawa was carrying a key to an empty locker? Have you been able to come up with any explanations that make sense?"

Suzuki stopped typing and looked up. She sat back in her chair, folded her arms and crossed her legs.

"Well, sir, we have to consider the question of whether or not Mr. Sekikawa knew that the locker was empty. That seems to be the fundamental question here. It's very strange to have a key to a locker that you know is empty, but it's not so strange to have a key to a locker that you are using to store something, and to have had the contents of the locker removed by somebody else."

Morimoto nodded.

"In that case," Suzuki continued, "the question would be who stole Mr. Sekikawa's belongings, and how did they steal them? The report says that there's no evidence that the locker was broken into, but of course, we can't be completely sure of that. Another possibility is that somebody managed to obtain a copy of the key."

"Yes, Suzuki. The stationmaster would have the master key to all of the lockers, wouldn't he? Isn't it possible that someone else could have got hold of such a key?"

"I suppose that it's possible, sir, but it would have had to have been somebody who knew what they were looking for, and they'd have had to have known which locker Mr. Sekikawa was using. There haven't been any reports of thefts from any of the coin lockers at Kurashiki recently. Therefore, if somebody did remove the contents from locker two hundred and three, I think that we can safely assume that whoever it was had found out which one of the lockers was Mr. Sekikawa's locker. And moreover, they'd also have presumably known exactly what was in the locker, exactly what it was that they were after."

"Hmmm…if somebody did remove the contents of the locker, would that be the same person who murdered Mr. Sekikawa? If it were the same person, then they wouldn't have needed to obtain a duplicate key. They could have just taken the key from Mr. Sekikawa after they'd killed him."

"Yes, sir, and that would seem to suggest that they are different people, because if somebody did take the key from Mr. Sekikawa, then there's no reason why they'd have returned the key to the corpse after opening the locker. On the other hand, if the locker had been emptied before the murder, it would be strange for the murderer not to remove the key from Mr. Sekikawa's pocket before leaving him lying in the alley. The murderer would realize that we'd find the key and that we'd find an empty locker. I think that it makes more sense to assume that the person who actually committed the murder didn't know anything about the key and the locker, or at least wasn't interested in them in any way. In other words, the murderer probably didn't know that Mr. Sekikawa had the key in his pocket at all."

Morimoto and Suzuki contemplated these ideas for a while. Suzuki looked down at her computer, and Morimoto brushed his hand through his hair and looked out of the window. Their office was on the corner of the building and Morimoto could look outside in two different directions. The door was in the corner of the office, at the intersection of the two interior walls, and the umbrella stand was next to the door. Along the wall to the right of the door hung a white board, and at the end of the wall there was a tall bookcase. The white board was fixed midway up the wall, and next to it was a tray of colored marker pens that Morimoto and Suzuki occasionally used to draw diagrams and maps when they were discussing cases.

To the left of the door, a tall potted plant stood on the floor, and next to that was Morimoto's desk. Morimoto sat with his chair between his desk and the wall so that he could look out both the window in the wall directly opposite him and the window on the wall to his right. Underneath the window to his right was a low cupboard with some small pots containing various cactus plants arranged along the top.

In the center of the office three desks were arranged together, two of them back to back, with the third positioned along one end of these two. Suzuki sat at one of these desks facing Morimoto. On another of the central desks there was an electric hot water maker that Morimoto and Suzuki used for making tea, and next to it there was a tray with some teacups, a teapot and a container of green tea. There were two pictures hanging on the walls of the office. One was a painting by Claude Monet of water lilies in a pond at the gardens at Giverny. The other picture was a Japanese woodblock printing made by Katsushika Hokusai. It was from the series *The Thirty-Six Views of Mount Fuji*, and it showed a small park in Tokyo with cherry blossom trees from where Mount Fuji could be seen in the distance.

After a few minutes silence, Morimoto resumed their discussion.

"As you pointed out, Suzuki, the essential point here is whether or not Mr. Sekikawa knew that the locker was empty. It's not at all unusual to be walking round carrying a key to a locker in which you, or somebody else, have deposited something. But it's very unusual to be walking around carrying a key to an empty locker. In fact, it's very unusual indeed. When unusual behavior like that is observed, when an inconsistency of that kind is discovered, it's almost always an indication that there's something else going on, something else that is still unknown. When those additional facts have eventually been revealed, it invariably turns out that they provide a very simple explanation for what may otherwise be a rather puzzling phenomenon."

Morimoto paused again. Then looking over at Suzuki he asked another question.

"By the way, Suzuki, do you think that it's possible that Mr. Sekikawa had a meeting arranged with someone from the syndicates on Thursday night?"

"Hmmm...I've been wondering about that possibility, sir. If Mr. Sekikawa did have a meeting arranged that evening, then in that case he might have been intending to give the key to the person that he was meeting—to the person from the criminal organizations, say, if that was who he was planning to meet."

"For example," Suzuki continued, "let's suppose that Mr. Sekikawa had been able to raise some money, and let's suppose that he was planning to pay back some of his debts to the syndicates. He could have left the money that he'd raised in the locker at Kurashiki station, and then perhaps he'd been intending to give the key to somebody from the syndicates. Perhaps he'd arranged a meeting with someone from the syndicates that evening in order to hand over the key."

"Why not just give them the money directly?" Morimoto argued.

"Yes, why not? Well, perhaps he didn't want to carry all of the money around with him. Or, perhaps it was some kind of a trick that he was playing. Maybe he didn't have the money. Maybe he was intending to give the syndicates the key to the empty locker, while pretending that the locker had the money in it."

They glanced at each other.

"That's a sure way to get yourself killed," Morimoto said. "After the syndicates find out that they've been tricked, I mean."

"Yes, sir. You're quite right, of course. The only other logical explanation would appear to be that Mr. Sekikawa deposited some money in the locker with the intention of handing the key to the syndicates. Then, afterwards, unknown to Mr. Sekikawa, somebody else other than the syndicates found out about it. And moreover, they must have come up with a way of removing the money from the locker. So then, Mr. Sekikawa had the key to the locker which he thought had the money in it, while in fact, the money had been removed and it was really an empty locker."

Morimoto looked out of the window thoughtfully. Suzuki poured them both some tea. She was taller than the average Japanese lady, but she was not as tall as Morimoto. She had a fairly slender figure, with straight black hair that was tied in a single bunch at the back of her head. Her face had a slightly oval shape with dark brown eyes and a small mouth with thin lips. She wore contact lenses in preference to glasses, and she was fond of using a light pink shade of lipstick that was the same color as the nail polish that she liked to use on the tidily manicured nails of her thin fingers. Other than the lipstick, however, she generally wore very little make-up.

On this particular day, she had come to the office wearing a dark-gray suit. Her skirt extended to just above her knees, and underneath her jacket she wore a white blouse. She was wearing clear stockings and medium heeled, black shoes that she could easily slip off while she was sitting at her desk. Every day, Suzuki arrived at police headquarters carrying her briefcase in her right hand, and with a black leather handbag with gold buckles slung over her left shoulder. She kept the handbag on the floor underneath her desk while she was working in the office. Sometimes she wore some simple forms of jewelry, and on this day she was wearing a thin silver necklace with a small pendant.

As Morimoto and Suzuki drank their tea, they continued to contemplate the puzzle of the empty coin locker, and they compared the possible explanations that they had discussed. After a while, Suzuki offered another explanation.

"Actually, sir, something else did occur to me."

"Yes, Suzuki?"

"Perhaps the reason why the locker was empty is that Mr. Sekikawa was planning to deposit something in the locker later on. What I mean is, perhaps he had the key with him so that he could go and put something in that specific locker later that evening, or the next day, perhaps. Or, another possibility is that maybe he was going to give the key to somebody else so that they could use the locker."

Morimoto scratched his head.

"That would be rather strange, wouldn't it? If the locker was going to be used in the future, then why not just find an empty locker at that point in the future when it was needed? If you give somebody else the key so that they can use the locker, then they'd first of all have to open it up before they could deposit their items, whatever they were. After that, they'd have to pay three hundred yen again to close it and lock it again."

"Yes, sir, it would be rather strange, I agree. The only sensible explanation would appear to be that it was really important to use that particular locker, or a similar locker of the same size. If it was really important to be able to use one of those lockers in the future, then you might be worried that they'd all be taken by other people when you needed to use one."

"Ah, so what you're saying, Suzuki, is that you carry the key with you, in effect reserving the locker, so that you're certain that you or somebody else will be able to use it at some time in the future."

"Yes, I suppose so," said Suzuki with a shrug. "Having the key would be a kind of guarantee that you could use the locker in the future when you needed to use it. Presumably, you'd need to use it for some very important purpose—so important that you aren't willing to take the risk of not being able to find a locker available when you need one."

"And actually, number two hundred and three is one of the large lockers. There aren't too many of them, I suppose," added Morimoto.

"Yes, that's right. But the problem is, sir, when I called the station this morning I checked up on this idea. I asked the stationmaster at Kurashiki how often the large lockers are all occupied. He told me that the large lockers are almost never all in use at the same time. In fact, he said that there's almost always quite a few of the large lockers available to be used at any particular time."

"Not everybody would know that though, Suzuki. Unless somebody had done a careful study of the lockers over a period of time, they're not going to be completely sure that they'd always be able to go to the locker room and be able to find a large locker that wasn't in use."

"That's true, sir."

Morimoto and Suzuki resumed their individual contemplations for a while and sipped their tea. Morimoto looked out of the window again at the dark gray sky and the incessant rain. Suzuki stared at her computer.

"Of course, sir," Suzuki began again, "we don't actually know whether the key really belongs to Mr. Sekikawa, do we? Perhaps the key really has nothing to do with Mr. Sekikawa. It's true that you found the key in his pocket on Friday morning, but that doesn't mean that Mr. Sekikawa had the key with him on Thursday. The key could have been planted on his body after he was murdered, for example, or it could have been given to him before he was murdered."

"Quite," murmured Morimoto. "I was thinking about that possibility as well."

CHAPTER 6

───────────▼───────────

Later that Saturday morning, Inspector Morimoto and Police Officer Suzuki were working at their desks when there was a sharp knock on the door and Sergeant Yamada strode into the office.

"I've managed to track down Mr. Sekikawa's girlfriend, sir. As you suggested, some of his colleagues at National Electronics knew her. I was told that they'd been together for about three years. Her name is Ms. Sakai and she lives in Takashima. Here's her address. I've just spoken with her on the phone, and she said that she'd be quite willing to talk to us. Would you like me to send a car for her, sir?"

Morimoto deliberated for a moment before replying.

"No, thank you, Sergeant. I think I'll go to Takashima myself to meet her. Would you like to come, Suzuki?"

"Very well, sir," Suzuki replied.

"Good," Morimoto said. "Sergeant Yamada, perhaps you could call Ms. Sakai again and inform her that we'll be right over?"

"I'll do that, sir," Sergeant Yamada replied.

A few minutes later, Morimoto and Suzuki put up their umbrellas and walked out of the police headquarters They rode the tram to Okayama station and boarded a train on the Sanyo Main railway line, just as they had done the previous day when they had visited Kurashiki. This time, however, they traveled eastwards in the opposite direction from Kurashiki.

When the train left Okayama station, it soon passed over the wide Asahi River that flowed southwards from the mountains in the northern regions of Okayama prefecture, through Okayama city, and into the Seto Inland Sea. That morning the river was high and was flowing rapidly on account of the daily rain. Immediately thereafter, the train passed over the smaller Hakken River, and three minutes after leaving Okayama station the train pulled into its first stop, the small Takashima station, where Morimoto and Suzuki stepped out of the carriage and raised their umbrellas again. The station exit was at the side of the platform, just adjacent to where they had stepped off the train. They gave their tickets to the ticket inspector as they walked off the platform and out of the station.

Ms. Sakai's apartment was only a short walk from Takashima station. It was in a more modest building than Mr. Sekikawa's apartment in Kurashiki, but it was nevertheless in a very pleasant and quiet location, with a rice field on one side. Morimoto knocked on the door of the apartment, and he showed his police identification card to Ms. Sakai when she appeared in the doorway.

"Good morning, Ms. Sakai. I'm Inspector Morimoto and this is Officer Suzuki. I believe that Sergeant Yamada called you from the station to say that we'd be coming?"

"Yes, that's right, Inspector. I've been expecting you."

Ms. Sakai was rather pretty and in her young thirties, Morimoto judged, but on this Saturday morning it was quite clear from her appearance that she had been under a lot of stress. The look on her face revealed a great sadness deep inside.

"Come on in, please."

Ms. Sakai led them into her apartment where they sat down in the living room. Morimoto could see that the modestly furnished apartment was rather small, as he had expected, but like Mr. Sekikawa's apartment it was very well organized and tidily arranged. Morimoto tried to offer some kind words of sympathy.

"I'm very sorry about Mr. Sekikawa," he said quietly. "This must be a very difficult time for you. I'm very sorry to have to trouble you at a time like this."

Ms. Sakai smiled softly and nodded her head.

"If you don't mind," Morimoto continued, "I hope that I might ask you some questions. It's just to help us in our investigation of Mr. Sekikawa's death."

"Yes, of course. I don't mind at all. I'll be more than glad to answer your questions."

"Thank you. I believe that you've known Mr. Sekikawa for about three years now, is that correct?"

Ms. Sakai nodded.

"Yes, we've known each other for around three years, I think. That would be about right."

"And did you sometimes stay at Mr. Sekikawa's apartment in Kurashiki?"

"Yes, I did. Recently I've been staying there quite often."

"When was the last time that you visited there?"

"Well, it was Wednesday evening, this last Wednesday. It was the night before Atsushi—Mr. Sekikawa, that is—was killed. I went to Kurashiki after work on Wednesday. We left his apartment together on Thursday morning. We took the train together from Kurashiki to Okayama station."

"I see," Morimoto said. "What did you do when you reached Okayama station that morning?"

"Well, Atsushi went to his office at National Electronics. He walked there from the station. And I took the train back here. I came back to my apartment."

"Did you see Mr. Sekikawa again on Thursday?"

Ms. Sakai paused.

"No, I didn't. The last time that I saw him was in the morning when we left each other at the station."

"So you didn't see Mr. Sekikawa on Thursday evening, then?"

Ms. Sakai shook her head.

"No."

"And did you talk to him on the phone at all on Thursday?"

"No."

Morimoto reflected for a moment before continuing.

"When you left Mr. Sekikawa at Okayama station on Thursday morning, what time would that have been?"

"Well, let me see. It would have been about fifteen minutes before nine, I think. As I said, he was on the way to his office. That's usually the time that he'd go to work."

"And about what time did you arrive at his apartment in Kurashiki? About what time did you arrive there on Wednesday evening, I mean?"

Ms. Sakai considered for a moment.

"Well, on that day it was about seven o'clock, I guess. Seven o'clock in the evening."

"And was Mr. Sekikawa there when you arrived?"

"Yes, he was. He was already there waiting for me. He'd arrived shortly beforehand, I think."

Morimoto paused again. He could see that Ms. Sakai was quite upset, and she also looked worried. Nevertheless, she still managed to maintain a calm and dignified composure. Morimoto felt a certain respect and admiration for her.

"I was wondering," Morimoto began again, "whether Mr. Sekikawa had been acting strangely or any differently lately? Did he seem particularly worried or agitated at all?"

Ms. Sakai shook her head slowly.

"No, not really, Inspector. He hasn't been any different lately. There wasn't anything unusual about him."

There was silence for a while and Ms. Sakai shifted in her seat.

"Do you know of anyone who might have wanted to kill him?" Morimoto asked. "Do you know of any reason for him to be killed?"

Ms. Sakai shrugged.

"Well of course he had money problems. I mean big money problems. Serious problems. I wish that I'd been able to help him in some way. He was always being hounded by those people, the syndicates. He didn't like to talk about it very much."

"No," Morimoto sympathized. "I can understand that."

Morimoto brushed his hand through his hair and he waited for a few moments before continuing.

"Did Mr. Sekikawa ever mention that they might kill him? Was he afraid that the syndicates might kill him? Did he ever mention that he'd been threatened in that way?"

"No, not really. Not that I can remember. As far as I can recall he never mentioned specifically that they'd threatened to kill him. But they might have done, though. If they had, it's something that he might not have wanted to tell me. I don't know."

Morimoto nodded.

"By the way, did any visitors come to Mr. Sekikawa's apartment on Wednesday night?"

Ms. Sakai shook her head.

"No, nobody at all. At least, not while I was there. It was just the two of us for the whole evening."

"Were there perhaps any telephone calls to the apartment, then?"

"Let me see."

Ms. Sakai thought for a few moments.

"Yes, there was one telephone call on Wednesday night. I remember it now."

"Just one?"

"Yes, just one."

"One telephone call to Mr. Sekikawa's apartment in Kurashiki?"

"Yes, that's right."

"What time was that?"

"Oh, I don't know exactly. It must have been sometime between nine and ten o'clock, I think."

"Do you know who it was from?"

"No. Atsushi didn't mention who it was from."

"I see. Was it a long phone call?"

"No, no. Very short I think. I don't know exactly how long it was, but it was very short. I'm sure of that."

"Did either of you make any telephone calls yourself that evening?"

Ms. Sakai thought about this question.

"Well I didn't. And I don't have any recollection of either of us making any calls, actually. As far as I know, Atsushi didn't make any calls that evening either."

Morimoto stroked his chin. Suzuki was watching Ms. Sakai closely.

"Well," Morimoto said, "as you know, Mr. Sekikawa's body was found on Friday morning, and we don't have any knowledge of his activities after he left his office on Thursday evening. Can you help us at all with that? Do you know what plans Mr. Sekikawa had for Thursday evening?"

"Well, as far as I know he didn't have any special plans. I expect that after leaving his office he returned to his apartment, unless he had plans to go out with his colleagues for a drink or for a meal. He may have been planning to stay late at the office. I don't know. His work has been very busy lately. He often worked late at his office."

"So you weren't planning to stay with Mr. Sekikawa in Kurashiki on Thursday night, then?"

"No, not that Thursday night. I worked at lunchtime that day. I have a job as a waitress at the Bamboo Haven, one of the restaurants near the castle. Afterwards, I came back here."

Morimoto was almost ready to leave, but he still had one important question remaining.

"One last thing, Ms. Sakai. Did Mr. Sekikawa have an umbrella with him on Thursday morning?"

Ms. Sakai looked surprised.

"An umbrella? On Thursday morning? Well, let me see. It was raining all of last week, wasn't it? It's the rainy season now. So he'd always have had his umbrella with him."

"Yes, but I wonder whether you specifically remember Mr. Sekikawa having his umbrella with him on Thursday morning at Okayama station? That was when you saw him for the last time, you said."

Ms. Sakai considered again.

"Yes, Inspector, I'm quite sure," she said slowly. "He did have his umbrella with him. As we parted he had his umbrella in one hand and he was carrying his briefcase in the other."

"What kind of umbrella did he have?" Morimoto inquired.

"What kind of umbrella? Well, I don't know. It was just an umbrella. What do you mean?"

"What color was it?"

"Green, dark green. Atsushi had a dark green umbrella."

"Was it the kind that folds up, so that you could put it inside a briefcase, for example."

"No, it wasn't that kind. He didn't like that kind of umbrella. It was the other kind, the kind that won't fold up. A real umbrella."

"Thank you."

Morimoto looked over at Suzuki.

"Well, I think that's all the questions we have, isn't it?"

Suzuki nodded. Morimoto and Suzuki stood up and Ms. Sakai showed them to the door.

"I'm very grateful for your help in our investigation, Ms. Sakai," Morimoto said. "I hope that it hasn't been too distressing for you."

Ms. Sakai shook her head.

"And please let me say again," Morimoto continued, "how sorry I am about what happened to Mr. Sekikawa."

"Thank you, Inspector."

As he walked out through the doorway, Morimoto turned and asked a final question.

"By the way, Ms. Sakai, did Mr. Sekikawa ever use a coin locker at Kurashiki station?"

Ms. Sakai looked startled.

"A coin locker at Kurashiki station? Well, he lives quite close to the station. I don't know why he'd ever need to use a coin locker there. At least, I've never known him to use one."

CHAPTER 7

―――――――――――▼―――――――――――

Inspector Morimoto and Police Officer Suzuki returned to police headquarters from Ms. Sakai's apartment in the same way that they had gone there, by train and tram. When Suzuki checked her computer back at the office, she found that some new information on the case had arrived.

"Sir, something new has come in. A life insurance policy on Mr. Sekikawa has been traced. I've got the details here on my computer. It's to be paid to his wife in Tokyo—all of it. It's a reasonable sum, sir, but nothing unusual."

"I see," Morimoto said as he sat down at his desk. "How recently was the policy taken out?"

"It's been quite a while, sir. The policy's been in effect for about eight years now."

"All right. That means that it was started before Mr. Sekikawa's wife moved to Tokyo, doesn't it?"

"Yes, sir, it does."

"What about the premiums? Have there been any irregularities with the payments?"

Suzuki checked her computer.

"There doesn't seem to have been, sir. Mr. Sekikawa has been paying the annual premiums on time. The last one was paid at the end of February this year."

"Hmmm…I see. With all of his money problems, he still managed to maintain his life insurance policy."

"Yes, it would appear so, sir."

"Which insurance company is the policy with?"

"One of the big ones, sir—Calamity Assurance."

"I see. Well, Suzuki, could you check the phone records of Mr. Sekikawa's apartment for last week, please. Ms. Sakai said that there was one call on Wednesday night—a short one. Find out where that was from, and see if there were any other calls on Thursday night."

"Yes, sir, I'll do that right away."

"And by the way, Suzuki, what did you think of Ms. Sakai?"

Suzuki frowned.

"Well, sir, she didn't look very comfortable. She was very nervous. It's difficult to tell, though, whether it's all due to her being upset over Mr. Sekikawa's death, or whether there's something else going on."

"Yes. Well, while you're at it, you'd better check Ms. Sakai's phone records as well. See whether there were any calls to or from her apartment on Wednesday and Thursday night, please."

"Very well, sir."

Morimoto leaned back in his chair and put his legs up on his desk as he tried to sort in his mind what he knew about the case. According to what Ms. Sakai had told him, Mr. Sekikawa had gone to work on Thursday morning as usual, and he had taken his umbrella with him. According to his colleagues at National Electronics, Mr. Sekikawa had left his office at about six fifteen, and then according to the pathologist Dr. Ogata, he had ended up having his throat slashed some time before nine o'clock that evening. His umbrella was not with his body when it was found, but he did have the key, the key to the empty coin locker.

The murder was either a syndicate killing, or it had been made to look exactly like a syndicate killing. There was a life insurance policy in his wife's name, a wife who claimed not to have met Mr. Sekikawa for five years. And Mr. Sekikawa had been heavily in debt to the syndicates for quite a while, and everybody seemed to be aware of it.

The syndicates certainly had a reason to harass Mr. Sekikawa, but would they actually go so far as to kill him? And then there was the matter of the company where he worked, National Electronics. It was under investigation from Tokyo for possibly leaking national secrets abroad. Did that have anything to do with Mr. Sekikawa's murder? What had Mr. Nishi's investigation of Mr. Ishihara's division uncovered? How closely was Mr. Nishi monitoring his own investigation into Mr. Sekikawa's murder?

As Morimoto contemplated these matters, Suzuki reported back with some information on the telephone calls.

"There doesn't appear to be anything unusual in the telephone records, sir, at least not as far as I can tell at the moment."

"What about the night before the murder?"

"Wednesday night, sir? Yes, there was one telephone call that night to Mr. Sekikawa's apartment in Kurashiki, just as Ms. Sakai told us there was. There were no calls made from the apartment. The call came in at 9:21 in the evening, and it lasted for exactly forty-four seconds. It came from a public telephone at Osaka railway station."

"Oh, I see."

"And on Thursday there were no calls either to or from Mr. Sekikawa's apartment."

"And what about Ms. Sakai's apartment?"

"No calls going in or out on either Wednesday or Thursday, sir."

"Well, the telephone records do agree exactly with what Ms. Sakai told us," Morimoto murmured as he stroked his chin. "A public telephone at Osaka railway station, you said. At 9:21—a short call. Who do we know who was in Osaka on Wednesday night?"

"Well, sir, there's Mr. Ishihara, of course."

"Yes, quite."

"And we had mentioned before that Mr. Sekikawa might have had a meeting arranged with the syndicates for Thursday night. It would be quite normal for them to call him from Osaka to arrange the meeting."

"Yes, that's a good point, Suzuki."

Morimoto resumed his contemplation. After a while, he looked over at Suzuki again.

"Well then, Suzuki, perhaps you could arrange to have the police in Tokyo interview Mrs. Sekikawa? Tell them it's just a routine matter. Ask them to find out what she was doing last week, and see whether she's made a trip to Okayama recently, or to Osaka, as well. Oh, and have them ask her whether she knew about her husband's life insurance policy, would you?"

"Yes, sir. I'll give Tokyo a call right away."

"Thank you, Suzuki. Oh, and another thing—Mr. Sekikawa's dark green umbrella. Ms. Sakai said that he had it with him when he went to his office on Thursday morning. Could you please get in touch with National Electronics and see if you can find out whether Mr. Sekikawa left his umbrella at his office on Thursday evening. If he did leave it there, then it ought to still be there. Or see whether there's somebody who remembers Mr. Sekikawa taking his umbrella with him when he left."

"All right, sir," Suzuki answered and stood up. "I'll check with Sergeant Yamada first about who we've spoken to over there."

Just as Suzuki was leaving the room, Morimoto called after her.

"Oh, and Suzuki…just a moment."

Suzuki stopped and looked back at Morimoto.

"Yes, sir?"

"One last thing. Perhaps you wouldn't mind checking up on Mr. Ishihara's business trip to Osaka, would you? Perhaps you could go over to National Electronics and find out some of the details from him."

"Very well, sir," Suzuki replied.

CHAPTER 8

▼

On Thursday morning, the week after the murder, Inspector Morimoto was leafing through the various reports on his desk that dealt with Mr. Sekikawa's murder case. One thing that interested him in particular was that Mr. Sekikawa's dark green umbrella had not been found in his office at National Electronics.

Police Officer Suzuki's investigation had revealed that upon arriving at work, Mr. Sekikawa always left his umbrella in the umbrella stand in the office that he shared with his colleagues, and Suzuki had checked that it was no longer there. The natural presumption, therefore, was that Mr. Sekikawa had left his office on the Thursday evening of his murder with his umbrella. It had, after all, been raining quite heavily that evening. However, none of Mr. Sekikawa's colleagues could remember seeing him leave with his umbrella.

Earlier that morning, Morimoto had asked Suzuki about the umbrella.

"Well, Suzuki, what do you think about Mr. Sekikawa's umbrella? Ms. Sakai said it was a dark green umbrella, didn't she? Where do you think it is now?"

"Well, sir, considered from a logical point of view, Mr. Sekikawa either lost it before he was killed in the alley, or the murderer took it. Probably, the former is more likely, I'd say. Of course, that's supposing that no passerby would steal an umbrella from a corpse. And also, it's assuming that Mr. Sekikawa was murdered at the place where he was found. He could in fact have been killed anywhere, and then his body could have been dumped in the alley afterwards. In that case, his umbrella may be at the location of his murder, or more likely perhaps, it may have simply been thrown away by the killer or killers."

"How would you throw away the umbrella of somebody that you'd just killed?"

Suzuki shrugged.

"Well, sir, since it might provide some clues to the murder you'd want to dispose of it carefully, somewhere where it wouldn't be found. You could throw it into the river, perhaps? Yes, if it were myself I'd throw it into the Asahi River, I think. It would sink, wouldn't it? You could always fill it with some stones to make sure that it would sink. Anyhow, if it didn't sink then it would be carried away in the flow very quickly, considering all the rain that we've been having. It would reach the Seto Inland Sea in no time at all."

Another report on Morimoto's desk was from the police in Tokyo who had interviewed Mrs. Sekikawa. She had repeated to the Tokyo police what she had said before when Suzuki had phoned her the day that the murder had been discovered. She said that she had not seen her husband for five years. However, Mrs. Sekikawa had also told the Tokyo police that she had been aware of the life insurance policy that Mr. Sekikawa held, and she had been aware that she was listed as the sole beneficiary.

With regards to her whereabouts at the time of the murder, Mrs. Sekikawa said that she had been at her home in Tokyo all of that week. Specifically, on Thursday night, the night of the murder, she said that she had been at home with her son. There had just been the two of them together. The Tokyo police had spoken to some of Mrs. Sekikawa's neighbors who had been able to confirm that they had seen Mrs. Sekikawa every day of the previous week, the week of the murder. Mrs. Sekikawa also said in the interview that she had not been to either Okayama or Osaka for several years.

Suzuki had also made a visit to National Electronics to interview Mr. Ishihara once again, and she had compiled a report on Mr. Ishihara's business trip to Osaka. On Wednesday morning, the day before the murder, Mr. Ishihara had been taken by taxi to Okayama station from his home in the northern suburbs of Okayama. The previous day his secretary had given him a reserved seat ticket for the Nozomi bullet train that had left Okayama station at 7:46 that morning.

The Nozomi had arrived at Shin-Osaka station at 8:28, and from there Mr. Ishihara had taken a taxi to the offices of Consolidated Chipboards, the contractors with whom he had business that day. It seems that he had reached their offices at about 8:50. Suzuki had also spoken to the chairman of Consolidated Chipboards who had verified that Mr. Ishihara had visited them that day. He had also confirmed that Mr. Ishihara was a frequent visitor, who usually came to Osaka at least once a month.

On the Wednesday evening, Mr. Ishihara's hosts at the contractors had invited him out for dinner. They had visited a restaurant in the downtown district of Osaka, and at the end of the meal Mr. Ishihara had left the restaurant by himself at about nine o'clock. He had left by taxi and was taken to the Crystal House Hotel where he checked in for the night.

The Crystal House Hotel was a standard type of hotel catering to businessmen on business trips. It was located near Osaka station. Mr. Ishihara's check in time of 9:30 Wednesday evening had been verified by Suzuki from the hotel records. Suzuki had also found out from the hotel records that Mr. Ishihara often stayed at the Crystal House Hotel on his business trips to Osaka.

Mr. Ishihara had spent the following day, Thursday, at Consolidated Chipboards, but he had left by taxi at about five o' clock and he had returned to his hotel. Mr. Ishihara told Suzuki that shortly after returning to his hotel, he had taken another taxi to the Osaka Dome to attend the baseball game that had started at six o'clock. After the game, Mr. Ishihara said that he had returned by taxi to his hotel.

Most professional baseball games in Japan take somewhere between three and three and a half hours to complete their full nine innings, or to complete the eight and a half innings which are sufficient to decide the outcome of the game if the home team is leading at that juncture. However, the game in the Osaka Dome that evening had been tied after nine innings, and so additional innings had been required. The game had been decided only after thirteen innings had been played, which had not been until 10:45 that evening. Mr. Ishihara had said that he had stayed in the Osaka Dome right until the end of the game.

Finally, on Friday morning Mr. Ishihara had checked out of the Crystal House Hotel at 8:35, and he had taken a taxi again to Consolidated Chipboards. He had been intending to return to Okayama that evening after spending the full day working with the contractors. However, at about eleven o'clock that morning he had received a telephone call from his company's headquarters in Okayama notifying him of Mr. Sekikawa's death.

Upon receiving this news, Mr. Ishihara had cut short the last day of his visit to the contractors. He had returned to Okayama earlier than he had planned by taking a Nozomi bullet train that afternoon. He had been met by a police car at Okayama station, and he had been driven to the police headquarters where Morimoto had met and talked with him.

Suzuki had also asked Mr. Ishihara about the short forty-four second phone call that Mr. Sekikawa had received at his apartment in Kurashiki on the Wednesday evening. Mr. Ishihara had said that he had not called Mr. Sekikawa's apartment from Osaka station that Wednesday evening. However, Suzuki had noted in the report that the phone call had been at 9:21 that evening. Therefore, theoretically, it would have been possible for Mr. Ishihara to have made the phone call from a public telephone at Osaka station before walking the short distance to the Crystal House Hotel in time to check in at 9:30, as the hotel records showed. Suzuki had also noted in her report that Mr. Ishihara was right-handed.

While Morimoto was reviewing these reports, Suzuki suddenly hurried into the office with an excited look on her face.

"I think that I've come up with something important, sir."

Morimoto looked up from the reports.

"Yes?"

"It's about Mr. Sekikawa's girlfriend, sir, Ms. Sakai. I've been looking into her finances. I've just been talking with Mr. Izumi, the branch manager of the Metropolitan Trust Bank in Takashima. That's where Ms. Sakai has her account—or actually, to be more exact, what I should say is, that's where Ms. Sakai used to have her account. Mr. Izumi was able to give me the details of her bank account, and strangely enough it seems that she closed it last week. It was on Thursday, the day of the murder in fact. At ten o'clock in the morning, she went to the bank in Takashima near to where she lives, and she withdrew everything that she had in the account. It wasn't actually very much money, but she took it all out in cash. She closed the account."

"Really?" murmured Morimoto.

"Yes, sir. And then she did something even stranger. I managed to discover that she opened another bank account on Monday of this week, four days after the murder. She opened her new account at a different bank, though. It wasn't at the Metropolitan Trust Bank."

"Did she put all of the money back?"

"Yes, she did, sir. She deposited almost exactly the same amount of money that she withdrew last week."

Morimoto pondered this new information for a few moments. He thought about his meeting with Ms. Sakai on the previous Saturday. She had not mentioned anything about this.

"Well, Suzuki, what do you make of it, then?"

"It's rather strange behavior, sir, but the obvious deduction would be that Ms. Sakai was intending to give the money to Mr. Sekikawa to pay back some of the debt that he owed the syndicates. The only thing is, though, the amount of money that she had—it's really nothing compared with the amount of money that Mr. Sekikawa apparently owed the syndicates."

"But it would have been more than Mr. Sekikawa had himself, wouldn't it? You checked his bank accounts as well, and you found out that he had practically no savings at all, isn't that right?"

"Yes, that's right, sir. The money that Ms. Sakai had in her bank account was certainly much more money than Mr. Sekikawa had himself."

"Anyway, Suzuki, let's suppose that the money was for the syndicates. Perhaps that's not so surprising, is it? We can presume that the syndicates investigated most aspects of Mr. Sekikawa's life, and so it's certain that they knew about Ms. Sakai. And therefore, it's reasonable to assume that the syndicates would have done some research into her bank account. They'd have known how much savings she had. So maybe the syndicates decided that they'd try to get her money. They might even have threatened her personally, or more likely, they might have threatened that something would happen to Mr. Sekikawa if Ms. Sakai didn't hand over her money to them. In any case, if Ms. Sakai really did withdraw her money in order to give it to the syndicates, what else does that tell us?"

"Well, sir, it might suggest several things. First of all, it's probably significant that the money was withdrawn on the precise day of the murder. We might, therefore, deduce that Mr. Sekikawa had an appointment to meet the syndicates that evening. We've discussed that possibility before. Perhaps Ms. Sakai was going to give her money to Mr. Sekikawa on Thursday evening, and perhaps Mr. Sekikawa was going to hand it over to the syndicates? Maybe Mr. Sekikawa had arranged to meet the syndicates in the alley where he was killed?"

"But it looks as though she didn't give him the money," Morimoto pointed out.

"Yes, that's right, sir. It would appear that she didn't give the money to Mr. Sekikawa because she was able to put it back into another bank account on Monday. Perhaps she met Mr. Sekikawa on Thursday to give him the money, but maybe he'd changed his mind? Maybe he decided that he didn't want to let the syndicates have her money?"

"Yes, that's possible."

"On the other hand, sir, perhaps Mr. Sekikawa did take her money to give to the syndicates, but after his death the syndicates were noble enough to return the money to her."

Morimoto smiled.

"Yes, I see what you mean."

"Ms. Sakai could have given the money to Mr. Sekikawa," Suzuki elaborated, "but then when he met the syndicates, perhaps something went wrong. Perhaps the syndicates had been bluffing all along. Perhaps they were just tricking him.

Perhaps all they really wanted to do was to get him into that alley. Anyway, for whatever reason, the syndicates could have killed him and taken the money. Maybe they returned the money to Ms. Sakai later, at the weekend perhaps. And maybe that's why Ms. Sakai went to open a new bank account on Monday."

"Very honorable of them," Morimoto mused.

Morimoto and Suzuki contemplated these ideas for a while in silence, before Suzuki offered another suggestion.

"Of course, sir, another possibility is that it was Ms. Sakai who changed her mind. Maybe she changed her mind about letting the syndicates have her money. I mean, maybe she withdrew her money on Thursday with the intention of giving it to Mr. Sekikawa that evening, but then perhaps she changed her mind later on. For example, she might have had an argument with Mr. Sekikawa when they met on Thursday evening. In any case, the result would have been that Mr. Sekikawa would have had to have met the syndicates empty-handed."

"Mr. Sekikawa would have promised them the money beforehand," Suzuki continued. "He'd have told them that he'd be delivering the money to them that evening. But then, when Ms. Sakai changed her mind, he wouldn't have had any money to give them. So maybe the syndicates lost their patience with him. That could be the reason why the syndicates decided to kill him."

Morimoto reflected for a while.

"And how does the key to the coin locker come into all of this, Suzuki? Does Ms. Sakai's money shed any light on that puzzle?"

Suzuki frowned.

"It's difficult to figure that out, sir," she admitted. "The empty coin locker is still rather a puzzle. However, it would perhaps fit in with the idea that Mr. Sekikawa was tricked by Ms. Sakai, or at least that Ms. Sakai changed her mind about the money. Maybe Ms. Sakai gave Mr. Sekikawa the key to the locker, and perhaps she told him that she'd put her money in the locker, whereas really the locker was empty, as you found out. The problem is, though, in that case she wouldn't have actually needed to withdraw her money from the bank in the first place. It only makes sense if Ms. Sakai changed her mind after she'd closed her bank account."

Morimoto looked out the window, and he could see that the sun had started to shine. The morning had been overcast and gray, but the rain had finally stopped and it was becoming even hotter outside. As the rainy season drew to a close, there would be more and more sunshine in Okayama as the hottest part of the year approached.

Morimoto looked over at Suzuki again.

"But you know, Suzuki, this new development does at least seem to imply that Mr. Sekikawa had a meeting arranged with the syndicates. And furthermore, it does seem to imply that it was a meeting that Ms. Sakai knew about."

"Yes, that's right, sir."

"And consequently, it suggests that Ms. Sakai has not told us everything that she knows about this matter."

"Yes, I think that's undoubtedly true, sir. If there was a meeting arranged and she knew about it, then there's a lot that she knows about that Thursday evening that she didn't want to tell us. And in any case, she didn't tell us about closing her bank account, and it's very difficult to believe that's not somehow related to the other events of last Thursday."

Morimoto leaned back in his chair and rubbed his chin.

"And I wonder, Suzuki, I wonder whether the phone call on Wednesday night had anything to do with it, the phone call from Osaka station. Perhaps that had something to do with arranging the meeting between Mr. Sekikawa and the syndicates. As you mentioned before, it wouldn't be unusual for the syndicates to call from Osaka, would it?"

"Not at all unlikely, sir."

"We know that Ms. Sakai was with Mr. Sekikawa on Wednesday night. In fact, she told us that she remembered the telephone call. If the call set up the meeting, then they could have made plans afterwards regarding Ms. Sakai's money. They could have decided that Ms. Sakai would withdraw her money, and they could have decided how they'd deliver it to the syndicates."

"It's possible, sir."

"Anyway, Suzuki, one thing's clear. It's clear that we're going to need to have another chat with Ms. Sakai."

"Absolutely, sir," Suzuki agreed.

CHAPTER 9

▼

For a while, Inspector Morimoto considered the possibility of sending a police car to fetch Ms. Sakai and bring her in for questioning. In the end, however, he decided on a more gentle approach. He looked at his watch. It was almost ten thirty. Police Officer Suzuki was typing busily on her computer.

"Suzuki? The restaurant where Ms. Sakai works—she said that it was the Bamboo Haven, didn't she?"

Suzuki stopped typing and looked up.

"Yes, sir. That's correct. It's near the castle."

"Would you call them and ask whether she's working today, please?"

"All right, sir."

Suzuki fetched the telephone directory from the bookcase and looked up the restaurant. She dialed the number, and after a short conversation she hung up the phone and looked over at Morimoto.

"Yes, they said that she's working today, sir, lunch and dinner. She hasn't arrived yet, but they're expecting that she'll be there before eleven thirty."

"Well then, I think that we'd better go over to the Bamboo Haven and have another little chat with her. How about it, Suzuki?"

"Good idea, sir."

A few minutes later, Morimoto and Suzuki boarded a tram outside the police headquarters that took them to Okayama station, where they transferred to another tram that delivered them a few streets from the castle. The sky was bright blue and the sun was shining brightly, but they had their umbrellas with them just in case there was an afternoon downpour.

The restaurant was only a few streets away from the tram stop, and as they entered they were greeted by a young lady in traditional Japanese dress—a light blue kimono with a decorative floral pattern, fastened around the waist with a wide sash that was dark red.

"Good morning," she said. "Are you here for lunch?"

"Actually, we'd like to speak to the manager, please," Morimoto replied.

"Oh, just a moment, please."

The young lady disappeared and returned shortly with the manager, a middle-aged lady wearing a business suit.

"Good morning," she said. "I'm the manager. How can I help you?"

Morimoto and Suzuki produced their police identification cards.

"I'm Inspector Morimoto and this is Officer Suzuki. I'm sorry to have to trouble you, but we were hoping to have a word with one of your waitresses, Ms. Sakai. We called a short while ago and were told that she'd be working here this morning."

The manager was clearly startled.

"Oh, I see. Well let me see if she's arrived yet. Just a minute, please."

The manager returned a moment later with an anxious look on her face.

"Ms. Sakai hasn't arrived yet, but she should be here soon. She's working lunch today. Perhaps you'd like to wait in here?"

The manager slid open the door to a small private room. Morimoto and Suzuki removed their shoes and left them with their umbrellas outside the room before stepping inside. The floor was covered with traditional tatami mats, woven from straw and rushes, and they sat down on thin cushions placed on the mats, next to a low table.

"I'll be back in a minute with some refreshments for you," the manager said.

The Bamboo Haven was the kind of restaurant that catered mainly to businessmen. In fact, it depended almost entirely on its regular clients from the nearby business district. These local businesses used the restaurant to entertain their guests, who were usually businessmen from the other companies that they had dealings with. Morimoto wondered whether this was where Ms. Sakai had met Mr. Sekikawa.

After a few minutes the manager returned and served them both a cup of green tea.

"I suppose that your visit has something to do with Ms. Sakai's boyfriend, doesn't it?" she asked. "That was such a terrible thing—his being killed, I mean. Ms. Sakai told us about it."

"That's right," Morimoto replied, "we're investigating Mr. Sekikawa's murder. Did you ever meet him?"

"Oh no, I don't remember ever having met him. I don't know much about him, in fact. Ms. Sakai didn't talk about her private life very much."

"How long has Ms. Sakai been working here?"

"Oh, let me see. About four or five years now, I think. She's very reliable and easy to get along with—such a nice person. It's really tragic that this has happened to her. I do hope that she's going to be all right. She's not in any kind of trouble herself, is she?"

Before Morimoto could answer there was a timid knock on the door. The manager stood up and slid the door open to reveal Ms. Sakai waiting outside. It was clear that she was surprised to see Morimoto and Suzuki, and she also looked apprehensive.

"Ah, Ms. Sakai," the manager said. "Good morning. Come in, please. This is Inspector Morimoto. He's asked if he could have a few words with you."

The manager turned to Morimoto.

"Well, I'll leave you to it, Inspector. I'll be around if there's anything else that you need."

"Thank you very much," Morimoto said as the manager left.

Ms. Sakai removed her shoes and entered the room, closing the door behind her. As he looked at her, Morimoto could still detect in her face the sadness that had been apparent when they had first met on Saturday, five days previously.

"Please sit down, Ms. Sakai," Morimoto said. "I expect that you remember Officer Suzuki."

Ms. Sakai sat down on the mat and nodded towards Suzuki.

"I'm really very sorry to turn up here so unexpectedly," Morimoto continued, "but I'd rather like to find out some more information from you. I hope that this isn't too inconvenient for you?"

"No, not at all," Ms. Sakai said quietly.

Morimoto looked at her.

"We've found out about your bank accounts, you see."

Ms. Sakai lowered her eyes and stared down at the mat. She let out a long deep breath. She did not say anything.

"You closed your bank account last Thursday," Morimoto continued. "That was the day when Mr. Sekikawa was killed. And then you opened another bank account on Monday, and you put all of your money back into it. That's right, isn't it?"

Ms. Sakai nodded.

"Yes, that's right," she whispered. "You're quite right."

Morimoto did not say anything else. Ms. Sakai stared down at the floor again. They sat in silence for a while. Then in a soft voice Morimoto began again.

"We've been wondering…we thought that perhaps Mr. Sekikawa had an appointment to meet with some of the people from the syndicates. We wondered whether perhaps he might have told you about it? Perhaps the two of you discussed the matter?"

Ms. Sakai was looking more and more worried. She appeared to be finding it difficult to decide exactly what to say. Eventually, she looked up at Morimoto and spoke in a steady clear voice.

"Yes, you're right, of course. Atsushi did have an appointment to meet somebody from the syndicates last week. I knew all about it. You see, he'd explained to me that he needed my money. He told me that he needed all of my money, my savings. So I was very worried. I was very worried about what might happen to him, worried about what the syndicates might do to him. That's why I agreed to let him have my money."

Ms. Sakai sighed, but she seemed to be much more at ease now that she had spoken.

"It was just after Atsushi had received the phone call on the Wednesday night. That's when we talked about it, and he asked me for my money. I told you about the phone call when we talked before. That was the evening before he was killed, when we were together in his apartment for the last time. I know I told you that he didn't tell me about that phone call. I'm sorry, but really he did tell me."

Ms. Sakai blushed and rubbed her forehead.

"He told me that the call was from one of the people in the syndicates, and he said that he had to meet that person the next day, in the evening. He said that I had to get all of my money, and he wanted me to give it to him on Thursday evening. He said that after I'd given him the money he was going to meet the person from the syndicates. We'd planned to meet at Okayama station. I was supposed to give the money to him that evening at Okayama station. That's why I took out all of my savings and closed my bank account on Thursday."

Ms. Sakai shrugged.

"Maybe you think I'm silly, but I had to help him. I was so worried about him."

After she had finished speaking, Morimoto waited a few moments before asking a question.

"What time did you meet Mr. Sekikawa at Okayama station on that Thursday evening, then?"

Ms. Sakai sighed again. She looked straight at Morimoto.

"Well, that's it, you see…he never turned up!"

Morimoto waited for her to continue.

"We were supposed to meet at about six thirty. That was the time that we'd arranged to meet, but he never came. I waited for him until past seven thirty, but he still didn't come. I became worried, so I left the station and I went home. I only found out the next day that he'd been killed. One of his friends from his office told me—somebody who I'd met before. He called me and told me all about it."

Morimoto paused again before asking his next question.

"That phone call on Wednesday evening, do you know where it was from?"

Ms. Sakai considered for a moment.

"No, he just told me that it was from somebody in the syndicates. He just told me that he'd arranged a meeting for the next day, and he told me that he needed to pay some money."

"Did Mr. Sekikawa let you know any details of the meeting? Did he tell you where he was going to meet the person on Thursday evening, for example? Or did he perhaps tell you at what time he was supposed to meet them?"

Ms. Sakai shook her head.

"No, he didn't. He didn't tell me anything like that. He didn't mention any details at all, really. He just asked me to meet him at Okayama station at about six thirty with my money."

"Did Mr. Sekikawa know how much savings you had? Did he know how much money there was in your bank account?"

"Yes, he knew. I'd told him before. He said that he needed all of it."

Ms. Sakai stopped and looked at Morimoto.

"I suppose that you're wondering why I didn't tell you about all of this before," she said. "I know that I should have told you, I really do. And I wanted to tell you everything, but I was very scared, you see. Scared of the syndicates, especially after what they did to Atsushi. I didn't want to get involved. I didn't want to mention the meeting that Atsushi had planned with the syndicates at all. I thought that they might come after me if I said anything about them to you."

After reflecting for a while on what Ms. Sakai had told them, Morimoto decided to finish the interview at that point.

"Well, Ms. Sakai, I can understand why this whole episode is very upsetting for you. But I don't think that you need to be worried about the syndicates any more. I don't expect that they've any reason to be troubling you now. It was Mr. Sekikawa that they were involved with. Anyhow, I'm glad that you've explained everything to us. Thank you for that. As I said, we're sorry to have troubled you again, and I'm sure that you need to get on with your work."

Morimoto and Suzuki stood up. Suzuki slid the door open and they stepped out of the room. After he had put on his shoes and picked up his umbrella, Morimoto turned around and looked at Ms. Sakai again, and he asked one final question.

"Incidentally, Ms. Sakai, since you hadn't been able to meet Mr. Sekikawa you obviously still had all of your money with you, and you had to put it back into a bank somewhere. Why didn't you go back to the Metropolitan Trust Bank? Why did you go to a different bank?"

Ms. Sakai looked embarrassed and shrugged.

"Well, I'd have felt rather silly going back to the same bank again. It was bad enough having to walk in there and take out all of my money in the first place. I've been using the Metropolitan Trust Bank for most of my life. I wonder what they thought when I closed my account?"

Morimoto and Suzuki returned to police headquarters by tram via Okayama station. They had not been sitting at their desks for very long when Sergeant Yamada knocked sharply on the door and stuck his head inside the office.

"Good afternoon, sir. The Chief called and left a message while you were out. He'd like you to go upstairs and give him an update on how you're getting on with Mr. Sekikawa's murder case. He's in now if you'd like to go on up."

As Morimoto rode the elevator up to the seventh floor, he straightened his tie and deliberated about what he should tell the Chief. The new information that they had just received from Ms. Sakai seemed to answer some questions, but there were still many points about the case that remained mysterious.

The Chief looked up from behind his desk as his secretary showed Morimoto into his office. Morimoto noticed that the Chief was alone. There was no sign of Mr. Nishi this time. The Chief's office was much larger than the one shared by Morimoto and Suzuki, and it was also considerably more cluttered. Besides the spacious desk behind which the Chief was sitting, which was almost completely covered with piles of documents and files, the additional furnishings included a large table with eight chairs, and a low coffee table next to a sofa. Three out of the four walls were hidden behind tall bookcases that were filled with smartly bound police journals and other reference materials.

"Ah, there you are, Morimoto. Thank you for coming up. Do sit down. Mr. Nishi and I were hoping that you could give us an update on your investigation…into the murder case…Mr. Sekikawa. What have you found out? Have you been able to make much progress?"

Morimoto sat down in front of the Chief's desk and he explained the status of the investigation, including the information that he had learned from Ms. Sakai that morning.

"So you see, sir," Morimoto concluded, "this new evidence from Mr. Sekikawa's girlfriend is very significant. It's very significant because it establishes a direct link between Mr. Sekikawa and the syndicates on that particular Thursday evening. It confirms that Mr. Sekikawa had planned to meet the syndicates on the very evening that he was murdered."

"Yes, yes, Morimoto, I can see that. And this new information would appear to fairly clear up the whole matter, wouldn't it? I mean, unless we can get anybody from the syndicates to talk to us, that is."

"Yes, sir. It would seem to very much clarify the matter, although, there are still some unanswered questions. For example, we don't know why Mr. Sekikawa didn't meet Ms. Sakai on Thursday night as they'd arranged. And in addition, there are perhaps some other little peculiarities about the case that remain."

The Chief looked surprised.

"What exactly do you mean, Morimoto?"

Morimoto explained about the empty coin locker that he had found at Kurashiki station, and he also mentioned the missing umbrella of Mr. Sekikawa. While the Chief was considering these matters, Morimoto took the opportunity to ask a question himself.

"By the way, sir, is Mr. Nishi away today?"

"Yes, he's back in Tokyo today."

"And how's his investigation going, sir?"

"Well you know that I can't go into that in any detail, Morimoto. It's very hush-hush, as I told you before."

The Chief lowered his voice.

"But let me just say, between the two of us, that I don't think Mr. Nishi's investigation will go on much longer. I think it's going to be wrapped up pretty quickly."

"Oh, that's very good, sir."

Morimoto pressed on.

"You said that it was a case of industrial espionage, sir, a matter of national importance. I was wondering if the syndicates might be involved in some way?"

"Ah, well, Morimoto, since you've brought the matter up, we do in fact know for certain that the syndicates are involved. We're quite sure of it."

The Chief gave Morimoto a wink.

"It's to do with chips, Morimoto—computer chips. That company, National Electronics, developed some new chips based on the latest technology. They're very high speed, or something like that. Anyway, the point is that it's very secret work. It's laying the foundations of our computer industry for the next decade. That's what they told me. As you can imagine, Morimoto, other electronics companies would give anything to take a look at those chips. So you can imagine the consternation when two of them went missing earlier this year! Special Branch was put on the case in a flash. It has to have been an inside job, in one way or another. We're convinced that there has to be somebody from the company who's involved in the theft."

Morimoto listened carefully and nodded.

"And then," the Chief continued, "one of the missing chips surfaced…overseas. We were very lucky there, I can tell you."

"Really, sir? What happened?"

"Very good work it was, Special Branch together with our overseas spy network. We intercepted the chip as it was being delivered abroad, just in the nick of time, as a matter of fact. We rather upset that foreign gentleman who'd paid so much money for it, I imagine. And, of course, we traced the payment and it led straight back to the syndicates. That's how we know that they'd been involved in selling the chip overseas. But we haven't managed to trace the money back any further than that, at least not yet. However, as I told you a moment ago, I'm confident that Mr. Nishi will have it all wrapped up very soon."

Morimoto pondered what the Chief had just told him.

"So what you're saying, sir, is that the syndicates sold one of the chips to somebody overseas, and received the payment for it."

"Yes, that's correct Morimoto, but the chip never reached the foreign fellow who paid so much for it."

"You mentioned that two chips went missing, didn't you, sir?"

"That's right, and we've recovered one of them."

"So the other chip is still missing, is it?"

"Err…well, yes. But I'm sure that it won't be going very far under Mr. Nishi's watchful eye."

"I see. And by the way, sir, was Mr. Sekikawa a suspect in Mr. Nishi's investigation?"

The Chief looked sharply at Morimoto.

"They've all been under suspicion, Morimoto," he said quietly. "All of the people in that division have been under suspicion."

Morimoto thought about the Chief's reply, and then he asked another question.

"That would mean that the division head, Mr. Ishihara, is also a suspect, wouldn't it, sir?"

The Chief did not reply.

CHAPTER 10

▼

After a leisurely breakfast at home with his wife on Thursday morning of the following week, two weeks after the murder had taken place, Inspector Morimoto arrived at Okayama station towards the end of the morning rush hour period. It was a clear sunny morning, and the weather forecast predicted sunshine and a hot day in Okayama, and also in Osaka, which was in fact Morimoto's destination that day.

He was wearing one of his favorite thin summer suits, and he carried only a small, light briefcase. He found himself in a happy mood that morning, and he viewed his approaching train ride and visit to Osaka with pleasant anticipation. The variation of a day trip of one kind or another to alter a daily routine is often sufficient to generate a certain amount of excitement, and moreover, it was not raining that day.

Morimoto could have reached Osaka in forty-two minutes by taking the Nozomi bullet train, but he was not in any particular hurry. Therefore, he allowed himself the luxury of taking the local trains running along the Sanyo Main railway line from Okayama to Himeji, and then with a change of train from Himeji on to Osaka. Instead of taking just forty-two minutes, it would actually take him closer to three hours to complete the journey. Almost anybody else would have regarded the Nozomi bullet train as the more luxurious alternative, but from Morimoto's point of view the local trains allowed him three hours of uninterrupted, relaxed thinking time. And in addition, the slow train ride along the Sanyo Main line passing through the countryside from Okayama to Himeji was one of Morimoto's favorite train journeys.

Morimoto bought his ticket at one of the automatic ticket machines on the first floor of Okayama station and passed through the ticket gate. He boarded his train at one of the nearby platforms. It was heading eastwards on the Sanyo Main line, and it was the same train that he had taken over a week before with Suzuki when they had gone to visit Ms. Sakai at her apartment in Takashima.

The four-carriage, electric powered train that Morimoto entered was among the most basic inventory of the Japanese railway company's rolling stock. It was painted dark green with a wide orange stripe along its sides. Morimoto placed his briefcase on the overhead rack and seated himself on one of the cushioned seats that were placed along the side of the carriage, parallel to the length of the carriage. He liked these seats because they afforded him a nice wide view out of the windows on the opposite side. The coolers and the ceiling fans in the carriage provided a welcome contrast to the early morning heat that had already built up on the platform outside.

Morimoto had only decided to make this trip to Osaka the previous day when he had been sitting in his office with Police Officer Suzuki. Most of that week they had been preoccupied with various other matters that had needed their attention, and there had not been any additional developments in the murder case of Mr. Sekikawa.

Nevertheless, Morimoto had been thinking about the case most of the time. He was unsatisfied with it, and by now he knew Suzuki well enough to know that she would also have been thinking about the case. Moreover, Morimoto expected that Suzuki had probably reached the same conclusions about the case that he himself had reached.

Morimoto thought back to his conversation with Suzuki the previous day.

"It's not that she's being completely untruthful, is it, Suzuki? It's more as though she's just not telling us everything."

Suzuki stopped what she was doing. She frowned, and looked over at Morimoto.

"Yes, I think that you're right, sir."

She had known at once to whom Morimoto was referring. He was, of course, talking about Ms. Sakai.

"Well then, tell me what your opinion is," Morimoto invited her. "What do you think about Ms. Sakai's account of what happened on that Wednesday and Thursday, two weeks ago?"

Suzuki took a deep breath.

"Well, sir," she started, "there are various aspects of the situation, as Ms. Sakai has described it, that are quite troublesome. First of all, I'd have to say that we must wonder whether Ms. Sakai's money would really have been of any interest to the syndicates. It's actually quite negligible in terms of the amounts of money that they're accustomed to dealing with. Perhaps more importantly, it's also quite negligible when compared with Mr. Sekikawa's debts to them."

"Therefore," she continued, "if the syndicates had decided to use Ms. Sakai as a source of money, they could much more profitably have forced her to take out a loan from her bank, say. They'd have quite easily been able to find out about her credit rating. I did in fact check into it myself. Mr. Izumi at the Metropolitan Trust Bank told me that Ms. Sakai is able to take out quite a substantial loan if she ever wants to. A much more sizeable amount of money than she has in her savings, at least."

"And of course, sir, we can expect that the syndicates would have been aware of that as well. And furthermore, it's clear that Mr. Sekikawa would have realized it also. In that case, why didn't Mr. Sekikawa just suggest to Ms. Sakai that she take out a loan from her bank? Ms. Sakai gave the impression that she was willing to do anything for Mr. Sekikawa. She was certainly willing to give him her savings, it seems, and so there doesn't appear to be any reason why she wouldn't have been willing to take out a loan for him."

Morimoto nodded.

"And another thing, sir," Suzuki continued, "we have no explanation of why, suddenly at this time, Mr. Sekikawa decided to use Ms. Sakai's money to pay back the syndicates. He could certainly have come up with the idea some time before, one might have thought. And the same can be said for the syndicates as well. If it was at their urging that Mr. Sekikawa had to use Ms. Sakai's money, then why hadn't they done that before?"

Morimoto rubbed his chin.

"Why do you think that Ms. Sakai didn't tell us the complete story the first time that we interviewed her?" he asked. "At that time, she didn't tell us anything about closing her bank account, she didn't tell us what the phone call was about, and she didn't tell us that Mr. Sekikawa had a meeting arranged with the syndicates. In addition, she didn't tell us that she was supposed to meet Mr. Sekikawa to give him her money. When we met her at the Bamboo Haven restaurant, she said that the reason why she hadn't told us everything at our first meeting was that she was scared of the syndicates. Do you think that she's telling us the truth? Is that really why she withheld so much information from us when we met her the first time?"

Suzuki frowned again.

"Well, of course, sir, the question of why Ms. Sakai wasn't very forthcoming when we spoke to her for the first time is obviously a key point. It could be argued, I suppose, that she really was afraid of the syndicates, and so that really is the correct explanation for her behavior. Who knows? Perhaps the syndicates had even contacted her directly? Perhaps they'd actually threatened Ms. Sakai herself?"

"On the other hand," Suzuki continued, "perhaps Ms. Sakai really did meet Mr. Sekikawa at the station, and furthermore, perhaps she did actually hand over her money to him. Then, afterwards, maybe something went wrong when Mr. Sekikawa met the syndicates, something that resulted in him being killed. And after that, maybe the syndicates returned her money to her, but told her to pretend that she didn't know anything about what had happened."

Morimoto scratched his head and nodded.

"Yes," he said, "you might be right. It's possible that Ms. Sakai gave her money to Mr. Sekikawa, and then the syndicates returned the money to her for some reason. And the syndicates might have insisted that Ms. Sakai deny meeting Mr. Sekikawa on Thursday evening, and therefore she'd have had to deny giving him the money."

"And," Suzuki added, "since Ms. Sakai indicated herself that she was at Okayama station on Thursday evening, we don't know for sure that she wasn't involved in the murder. Perhaps she met Mr. Sekikawa, and perhaps they left the station together, and perhaps they even went to the alley together, the place where Mr. Sekikawa was found dead. Perhaps Ms. Sakai even saw the murder taking place."

"It's certainly possible," Morimoto agreed.

"There's something else that's rather strange about Ms. Sakai's account, sir. She never called Mr. Sekikawa's apartment to find out if he was there. She never called him to find out why he didn't turn up at Okayama station as they'd arranged. She says that they were supposed to meet at six thirty, and that she waited at the station for him until after seven thirty. You'd think that she might have called his apartment in Kurashiki from the station to see if he was there."

Morimoto nodded.

"Also, sir, after she gave up waiting for him and went back to her apartment in Takashima, it would again have been natural for her to call his apartment to find out what was going on. But from the phone records, we know that no calls were made from her apartment that night, and that no calls were made to Mr. Sekikawa's apartment that night either."

As he sat in the train at Okayama station, Morimoto thought about his two meetings with Ms. Sakai. He thought about the kind of person that she had appeared to be. He remembered how upset and sad she had seemed on both occasions. She did not appear to be the sort of person who would get herself into trouble, she did not appear to be the sort of person who would mislead the police, and she did not appear to be the sort of person who would get herself mixed up in murder. Nevertheless, by her own admission, she had not told the truth the first time that they had met, and he now felt certain that the same could also be said for the second time that they had met.

As he pondered these matters, the train quickly filled up with high school students on their way to school, dressed in dark blue and black summer uniforms. When the seats had all been taken, the students filled the aisle of the carriage, and the noise level increased abruptly with their adolescent chatter and their hasty cramming of the previous evening's neglected homework.

After a brief warning siren had sounded, the train doors banged shut and the train jolted away from the platform. As it gathered speed, it left behind the downtown area of Okayama city, and it crossed over the Asahi River followed soon after by the Hakken River. The first stop was reached after only three minutes. It was Takashima station near to where Ms. Sakai lived, and even more high school students climbed on board.

After that, there were several stops in rapid succession, and at each of these additional passengers, including more students, squeezed into the crowded railway carriage. Eventually, the train pulled into a station on the outskirts of Okayama where the horde of high school students descended from the train en masse, and headed off to their morning classes at the nearby high school.

Morimoto's carriage was now empty except for a handful of individually seated passengers, and the only sounds in the carriage were the rattles and the bumping of the train itself as it rolled along the track. Presently it passed into the countryside, and Morimoto had an uninterrupted view across the empty carriage and through the opposite windows of the rural scenery of first Okayama prefecture, and then the neighboring Hyogo prefecture, with their steep hills and meandering rivers, mixed with fertile agricultural areas and dotted throughout with small farming villages.

Looking out at the rice fields, Morimoto could see the sturdy green rice plants sprouting up through the water in tidy symmetrical rows, with dragonflies hovering busily overhead. These images of rice fields in the summer had always had a calming influence on Morimoto. The orderliness and the precise arrangement of the rows of plants seemed to Morimoto to epitomize humanity's harmonious collaboration with nature. Morimoto also watched dark green hillsides covered with pine and cedar trees pass by. There were also forests of tall cypress trees, and lighter patches of green that were thick bamboo groves.

At the simple country railway stations where the train pulled into for just the briefest of stops, Morimoto watched some of the elderly village folk resting in the shade on the station benches placed along the edges of the platforms. As the train moved deeper into the countryside, Morimoto noticed smoke rising from wheat fields as the farmers cleared and burnt them, and soon the railway line ran alongside and crossed over fast-flowing, wide rivers, where Morimoto spotted anglers engaged in their patient battle with the large, black bass fish.

Morimoto was enjoying his train ride.

CHAPTER 11

▼

Rocked by the gentle rhythm of the train ride, Inspector Morimoto continued to ponder the murder of Mr. Sekikawa, and he thought back again to his conversation with Police Officer Suzuki the previous day.

"But, Suzuki, according to Ms. Sakai's account, she'd arranged to meet Mr. Sekikawa at Okayama station on Thursday evening. However, Ms. Sakai also claims that Mr. Sekikawa didn't turn up for that meeting. In fact, she says that she never saw him again. If she's telling us the truth, why do you think that Mr. Sekikawa didn't turn up for the meeting?"

"I've been wondering about that, sir. It's an important point, although there are perhaps some reasonable explanations. One possibility is that Mr. Sekikawa was intercepted by some syndicate members after he left his office. Perhaps they accosted him while he was on his way to Okayama station, and perhaps they took him away somewhere. That could be why he wasn't able to keep his meeting with Ms. Sakai."

"In addition," Suzuki added, "if there had been any kind of a scuffle when he was confronted by the syndicate members on the way to the station, then that could have been the moment when he lost his umbrella, his dark green umbrella which we haven't been able to find."

Morimoto nodded.

"On the other hand," Suzuki continued, "perhaps Mr. Sekikawa just simply changed his mind about meeting Ms. Sakai. Perhaps Mr. Sekikawa just decided by himself on Thursday that he didn't want to use Ms. Sakai's money after all. Perhaps, after thinking the matter over, he decided that he didn't want to get Ms.

Sakai involved with the syndicates, and that could be the reason why he didn't turn up for his meeting with her that evening."

As Morimoto watched the scenery passing by the train windows, he noticed long, glass greenhouses on the lower slopes of the hillsides. He knew that they were for growing the Muscat grapes that thrived in the hot summer climate once the rainy season had finished. As he had hoped, the pleasant train ride was providing him with the opportunity to contemplate the various aspects of the murder case that still perplexed him, and his mind soon returned to his discussion with Suzuki the previous day and the main puzzle of the murder investigation, which was the question of the empty coin locker.

"You know, Suzuki, there's one essential point to this case which needs to be resolved, and that's the key that we found in Mr. Sekikawa's pocket, the key that belonged to the empty coin locker. It seems to me that until we can find an explanation for the empty coin locker, then we're never going to be able to completely understand what really happened that evening."

Suzuki nodded.

"Yes, sir. The resolution of the puzzle of the empty coin locker is a very critical point."

"There are perhaps some possibilities with regard to that key, aren't there, Suzuki? Some possibilities that we didn't discuss before?"

"Yes, that's right, sir."

Morimoto looked at Suzuki.

"Have you perhaps thought about a possible key switch, Suzuki?"

Suzuki smiled.

"Yes, sir. A key switch. I have been thinking about that possibility."

Morimoto was pleased to hear that Suzuki had also realized that there might have been a key switch, but he was not at all surprised. In the short period that they had been working together he had already gained a great confidence in Suzuki's abilities as a detective.

"How do you think that it would have worked then, Suzuki?"

Suzuki took a deep breath and sat back in her chair facing Morimoto. She folded her arms and crossed her legs.

"Well, sir, the essential point about the coin locker keys is that…well, most of them look exactly the same. They're all short thick keys with yellow plastic number tags. No matter which railway station you go to, the coin locker keys all look similar. In fact, sir, I did make a point of checking the coin lockers at Okayama station. There's also a number two hundred and three locker there, and the key and the plastic tag do look exactly similar to the key to the locker at Kurashiki station, the key which was found on Mr. Sekikawa's dead body."

Morimoto nodded approvingly. He had also investigated the similarity of the keys in the coin lockers at Okayama station and Kurashiki station.

"In fact," he said, "it's also interesting to note that locker two hundred and three at Okayama station is also one of the large lockers, isn't it?"

"That's right, sir. It's exactly the same size as locker two hundred and three at Kurashiki station. And the point would be, sir, that by just looking at the two keys you wouldn't be able to distinguish the key from the locker at Kurashiki station from the key to the locker at Okayama station. They'd both have the same number on their yellow plastic tag, so they'd look exactly the same. However, they'd be completely different keys. Each key would only open its own locker."

"So that raises a lot of possibilities for what might actually have happened, sir. For example, let's suppose that Mr. Sekikawa had deposited something in locker two hundred and three at Okayama station. And let's suppose that he was carrying the key to that locker. Then it's possible that somebody else could have obtained the key from locker two hundred and three at Kurashiki station, and they wouldn't have deposited anything in the locker, they'd only have wanted to have the key."

Morimoto nodded.

"Then somehow," Suzuki continued, "that person managed to switch their key with Mr. Sekikawa's key from Okayama station. Mr. Sekikawa wouldn't have noticed the difference. He'd just have had a key for a number two hundred and three locker. He'd have thought that it was for the locker at Okayama station where he'd deposited his belongings, whereas really it would have been the key to the empty coin locker at Kurashiki station."

"And that's how you found him after he'd been murdered, sir. You found Mr. Sekikawa with the key to the empty coin locker at Kurashiki. After the two keys had been switched, the person who switched the keys would have been able to empty Mr. Sekikawa's belongings from the locker at Okayama station."

"It's a very interesting possibility," remarked Morimoto, "although I believe that there are two rather important associated points which need to be considered. Firstly, the person who switched the keys would have needed to know the number of the locker that Mr. Sekikawa was using. That's because the person would have wanted to be able to get the same number key from Kurashiki station, or from some other station. As far as we can tell, the duplicate key wouldn't necessarily have had to have come from Kurashiki station, would it?"

"No, sir. It could have come from any station, actually. And strictly speaking, the duplicate key wouldn't necessarily have needed to be the same number as Mr. Sekikawa's key, but it would have been more risky if it were a different number. That's because Mr. Sekikawa might have remembered the number of his key, and therefore he might have noticed the key switch. Consequently, it would have made sense to try to obtain a duplicate key with the same number."

"Yes, I agree, Suzuki. And the second point which needs to be considered is that the person who switched the keys would have needed to be able to find another vacant locker of the same number somewhere else. Even though we discovered that there are always empty lockers available at Kurashiki station, for example, that doesn't imply that a locker of a specific number will always be available at a specific time."

"Yes, that's correct, sir. In order to carry out the switch, the person, whoever it was, would first have needed to know the number of the locker that Mr. Sekikawa was using, and then they'd have needed to be able to find a key with the same number at another station."

After a pause, Suzuki added another thought.

"And, sir, a key switch might offer an explanation for why Mr. Sekikawa was murdered. Let's suppose that Mr. Sekikawa had deposited some money or some other valuable items in locker two hundred and three at Okayama station. And then let's suppose that he did meet the people from the syndicates on Thursday night and that he handed them the key, except that unknown to him, it was actually the key to a different locker."

"It's not unreasonable to assume, sir, that the syndicate members would have taken Mr. Sekikawa with them to the locker in order to make sure that it really had the money inside it, or whatever else it was that he'd promised them. They'd have all gone together to the locker at Okayama station."

"But when they arrived there," Suzuki continued, "and when they tried to open up the locker, they'd all have been rather surprised. They'd have discovered that the key wouldn't open the locker. It's not hard to imagine that the people from the syndicates might have become quite angry with Mr. Sekikawa. I'm sure that they'd have thought that he'd been trying to trick them."

"And that could be the reason why they killed him," added Morimoto.

"Exactly, sir."

Morimoto's train passed through small farming villages, on the outskirts of which were small graveyards dug into the hillsides. The small, individual stone tombs were square in shape, with rectangular stone blocks set above them. Many of them had flowers and green branches laid out in front of them. Morimoto occasionally noticed small Buddhist and Shinto temples on the hillsides, with large entrance gates behind which stretched long series of steps leading up to the main temple buildings.

As his ride progressed, Morimoto also looked out at spacious orchards, many of them growing peaches for which Okayama prefecture was well known. When the train stopped briefly at the small railway station in the village of Mitsuishi, Morimoto could see the brown, brick pottery ovens located throughout the village, which produced a distinctive pottery, famous throughout the region. Each oven had a tall, square brick chimney held together by metal bands, and those that were in use were discharging plumes of white smoke up into the blue sky.

After leaving Mitsuishi, the train became enclosed in darkness as it passed through a tunnel beneath one of the surrounding hills. Eventually, it emerged into the sunshine on the other side of the hill, and before long it began to approach the city of Himeji. Leaving the countryside behind it, the railway line began to thread its way between factories and residential areas again.

Morimoto's carriage filled up to the point where the seats were all occupied once more, and the aisles became crowded with standing passengers. Finally, an announcement over the carriage intercom system indicated the train's imminent arrival at Himeji station. It also provided information for Morimoto regarding which platform to go to for his connecting train to Osaka.

CHAPTER 12

▼

As his train approached Himeji station, Inspector Morimoto glanced out of the left hand side of the carriage, and in the distance he was able to see the majestic white form of Himeji castle, probably the most beloved of all Japanese castles. After the train had stopped and the carriage doors had opened, Morimoto stood up and retrieved his briefcase from the overhead rack. He stepped off the train onto the crowded platform and made his way down the stairway that led to the underground passageway linking the platforms. He walked along the passageway and ascended the stairs to the platform for Osaka bound trains. He was just in time to step aboard the waiting express train before the doors closed and it accelerated rapidly away, racing along the tracks towards Osaka.

As he settled into his new seat, Morimoto thought back again to the previous day's conversation with Police Officer Suzuki.

"Well, Suzuki, let's continue to explore the hypothesis that there were actually two coin locker keys, and that they were switched at some point. Who do you think would have switched the keys?"

"Well, sir, the primary suspect would, I suppose, have to be Ms. Sakai. From what we know, she's the person who'd have been in the best position to be able to find out about Mr. Sekikawa's plans. And moreover, she's the person most likely to have had an opportunity to switch the keys."

"For example," Suzuki continued, "one possible scenario is that somehow Mr. Sekikawa had been able to raise some money, and let's suppose that he'd put it in a locker at Okayama station on Wednesday, say. He could have told Ms. Sakai about it that evening when they were together in his apartment at Kurashiki. And

Ms. Sakai would have been able to see the coin locker key that he'd obtained, if she'd wanted to. She'd have been able to see what number it was, for instance."

"Then, sir, it seems plausible that the phone call to Mr. Sekikawa's apartment that evening did have something to do with the syndicates. Specifically, let's suppose that during the phone call that evening, Mr. Sekikawa really did arrange a meeting on Thursday night with the syndicates. Then, maybe Ms. Sakai did meet Mr. Sekikawa at Okayama station on Thursday evening—presumably she'd have met him before his meeting with the syndicates—and she'd have had the whole day to obtain a duplicate key. So it's possible that Ms. Sakai managed to switch the keys when she met Mr. Sekikawa in the evening. Obviously, when Mr. Sekikawa gave the syndicates the wrong key and they found out that they couldn't open the locker at Okayama station, they wouldn't have been very happy with him. Anyway, when the coast was clear, Ms. Sakai could have emptied the locker herself."

Morimoto rubbed his chin.

"Yes, I see what you mean," he said. "But that would mean that Ms. Sakai was deliberately double-crossing Mr. Sekikawa, wouldn't it? Furthermore, it would mean that she was practically sentencing him to death as well. Ms. Sakai must have realized that it would be very probable that Mr. Sekikawa would be killed when the people from the syndicates found out that the money wasn't there—when they came to the conclusion that Mr. Sekikawa had been trying to trick them."

"Yes, that's right, sir. In fact, Ms. Sakai would probably have been relying on Mr. Sekikawa being killed. That's because, otherwise, she'd have known that Mr. Sekikawa would have been able to guess that it was she herself who'd tricked him. He'd have been able to work out that it was she herself who'd switched the keys. So she'd have realized that if Mr. Sekikawa had stayed alive, then she'd never have been able to get away with it unless she ran away somewhere and disappeared."

"Come to think of it, sir, it's quite possible that Mr. Sekikawa had been having death threats from the syndicates. And it's probably quite likely that he'd have told Ms. Sakai about them. Perhaps they both knew that this was his last chance to stay alive. Perhaps they both knew that his last chance was to make that payment to the syndicates, and perhaps Ms. Sakai saw an opportunity to take the money herself."

Morimoto scratched his head and he thought about his meetings with Ms. Sakai. He considered whether Ms. Sakai seemed to be the kind of person who could have done that to Mr. Sekikawa. She might have wanted to end her relationship with Mr. Sekikawa. He could believe that. But would she really have gone so far as to be involved in his death?

"There's something else that we need to consider, Suzuki. If that's what happened, then why did Ms. Sakai withdraw her savings from the bank?"

"That's a good question, sir. It's not clear why she'd have done that, but it's possible that it might have been a smoke screen."

"A smoke screen?"

"Yes, sir. A smoke screen for our behalf. Ms. Sakai would certainly have realized that she might be seen by somebody at Okayama station on the Thursday evening—seen by somebody who knew her, I mean—somebody who'd recognize her. So in that eventuality, she'd have wanted to be able to explain to us why she'd been waiting at the station. She'd have wanted to have a good reason why she'd been at Okayama station. Therefore, maybe that's why she decided to withdraw her money from the bank. Perhaps she wanted to be able to tell us that story, the story that she was at the station so that she could hand over her savings to Mr. Sekikawa."

"And what if she'd been recognized while she was with Mr. Sekikawa?" Morimoto asked. "Ms. Sakai must have actually met Mr. Sekikawa in order to switch the keys."

Suzuki shrugged.

"Well, if somebody had seen her with Mr. Sekikawa, then maybe Ms. Sakai was planning to give us a different story. In that case, perhaps she'd have told us that she'd given her savings to Mr. Sekikawa as she'd arranged, but that she hadn't heard from him again since then. And, of course, in that case she wouldn't have returned the money to a bank on the following Monday."

Morimoto gazed out of the window. It was raining again, but not too heavily that day, just an on and off drizzle. He was impressed and pleased with how far Suzuki had thought the matter through. The murder case seemed to be far from simple, yet at the same time it seemed to him that it was in some ways starting to become clearer. He had a sense that they might be on the right path. He felt that they were gradually getting closer to the truth, closer to understanding what had really happened on that Thursday evening when Mr. Sekikawa had his throat viciously slashed.

"And there's another question, Suzuki," Morimoto began again. "If Mr. Sekikawa really did put something in a coin locker somewhere, something valuable that was intended for the syndicates, what do you think that it would have been? Would he have just put money in a coin locker?"

"He might have, sir. If it was a lot of money, then he might have thought that it was safer to put it in a coin locker instead of carrying it around with him. If he hadn't used a coin locker for the money, then he might have had to keep the money with him all day on Thursday, all of the time that he was at his office."

"In any case," Suzuki continued, "Mr. Sekikawa might have thought that it was much easier, less conspicuous perhaps, to hand the syndicates the key to the coin locker rather than handing them the money directly. After all, sir, the coin lockers are very safe and anonymous. There are hardly ever any reports of thefts from them."

Morimoto pondered for a few moments.

"I've been wondering, Suzuki, whether there may be a direct connection here with the leaking of the secret materials from Mr. Sekikawa's company, National Electronics. We've been told that Mr. Sekikawa was a suspect. Suppose that Mr. Sekikawa was responsible for the leaks. Suppose that he'd stolen the two computer chips that went missing. He could also have made copies of some documents relating to the chips—plans, diagrams or something like that. Perhaps that's what he'd have wanted to store in a coin locker? Perhaps he used a locker to store some documents, or the computer chip that is still missing, with the intention of passing them on to the syndicates?"

"Yes, that's perfectly possible, sir. In effect, he'd be selling the company's secrets to the syndicates. Using the company's secrets, that is, as a means of canceling some of his debts to the syndicates. The syndicates would take the documents and chips from Mr. Sekikawa in place of the money that he owed them, and then they'd be able to sell the materials themselves. It certainly makes the use of a coin locker more reasonable though. Mr. Sekikawa wouldn't have wanted to keep the copies of the documents or the stolen chip with him at work."

Morimoto nodded slowly.

"Yes," he said, "and we shouldn't forget that we've been told that one of the chips almost reached a buyer overseas, and that the syndicates were involved in the deal. The payment was traced back to the syndicates. That would seem to imply that if Mr. Sekikawa was responsible for the theft of the chips, then he'd done this before. It would imply that he'd already given one of the chips to the syndicates."

"And if that is the correct scenario, sir," Suzuki added, "then presumably the syndicates were quite willing to take another chip from Mr. Sekikawa. After all, from their perspective, the first chip had worked out very well for them. It had been a very lucrative deal, from what we've been told."

"Yes, that's right, Suzuki. Rather unpatriotic criminals, wouldn't you say?"

"Very much so, sir."

They continued drinking their tea for a while and then Suzuki made another suggestion.

"Incidentally, sir, if the syndicates were selling the secret materials abroad, then it would be much easier for them to arrange it all from Osaka, much easier than it would be to arrange it here in Okayama."

"Yes, you're probably right."

"And perhaps, sir, that would explain why the phone call came from Osaka— the phone call to Mr. Sekikawa's apartment on Wednesday evening that Ms. Sakai told us came from the syndicates."

Morimoto had a window seat on the right hand side of the express train from Himeji to Osaka. Not long after leaving Himeji station, the railway track ran alongside the Seto Inland Sea that separates the Japanese mainland from the island of Shikoku, and Morimoto's seat afforded him an uninterrupted view of the water. The sea was quite calm that day, and Morimoto could see oyster nets floating in the water close by the shoreline. Further out to sea were small fishing boats and larger cargo boats heading eastward, like the train, towards the ports in Kobe and Osaka just a little further up the coast.

As Morimoto's express train sped through Akashi station, he looked out at the two enormous towers rising out of the water that supporting the double-decker suspension bridge linking the mainland with Shikoku, and soon thereafter the train passed through the city of Kobe, crammed onto a narrow strip of land between its busy port on the southern side and mountains on the northern side. The train stopped at two stations in Kobe before setting off on the final leg of its journey to Osaka.

Morimoto closed his eyes for a while and contemplated the murder case again. He knew that there were quite a few facts that they were not yet aware of. The previous day he had wondered whether he should question Ms. Sakai again, right away. He was sure that there was a lot more about the case that Ms. Sakai had not told them. Was it the right time to confront her? Would she change her story again?

However, he had also been thinking about Osaka, and he knew that there was somebody else who visited Osaka often—Mr. Ishihara, Mr. Sekikawa's superior at National Electronics. After careful consideration of the matter, he had eventually decided that before talking to Ms. Sakai again, he would first visit Osaka.

As his train approached Osaka station, he began to wonder what new information he would be able to obtain there that day.

CHAPTER 13

▼

After leaving Kobe, it was not long before Inspector Morimoto's express train arrived at Osaka station. This large, busy station is located at the northern side of the central downtown area of Osaka, and it is the main railway hub of the city. However, the bullet trains pass through the more modern Shin-Osaka railway station that is located slightly to the north of Osaka station across the wide Yodo River.

With briefcase in hand, Morimoto exited the train and surrendered his ticket at the automatic gate as he left the platform. As he walked through the crowded station, he glanced over at a row of public telephones, and he wondered whether it was from one of these phones that Mr. Sekikawa's apartment had been called the night before his murder. He stepped into the noise and bustle of the pedestrian concourse outside the railway station building, and he stopped for a moment to get his bearings before heading along one of the main streets leading away from the station. The air was full of the clamor and exhaust fumes of the traffic, and after walking for a few minutes, Morimoto was glad to spot his primary destination for that day, a building with a large green sign that read Crystal House Hotel. It was the business hotel where Mr. Ishihara stayed on his trips to Osaka.

As he walked up the steps to the hotel entrance, the automatic glass doors slid smoothly open. Morimoto found the air-conditioned environment inside the hotel a welcome relief from the heat and humidity outside, and he looked around the hotel lobby. He noticed that the main reception desk was located on the far side of the lobby, opposite the main entrance doors through which he had just entered. He also observed that the elevators to the rooms were situated over to one side of the reception desk, and were in full view of the receptionists.

Morimoto walked across the shiny, marble floor to the reception desk and introduced himself to one of the receptionists, who was smartly dressed in a bright blue uniform.

"Good afternoon. I'm Inspector Morimoto from the Okayama Police Department. I have an appointment to see the hotel manager, Mr. Watanabe."

"Good afternoon, Inspector Morimoto," the receptionist replied. "Mr. Watanabe is expecting you. I'll show you to his office right away."

The receptionist took Morimoto to the hotel manager's office located at the end of a short corridor leading off from the main hotel lobby. As Morimoto was shown into the office, the hotel manager rose quickly from his seat to welcome him, and they both bowed politely to each other. Mr. Watanabe was in his early sixties, rather short and heavily built, with thinning hair. He was wearing a dark suit and he seemed a little nervous about Morimoto's visit.

"Good afternoon, Inspector Morimoto. I'm Mr. Watanabe, the hotel manager. It's so nice to make your acquaintance. Please do sit down. I hope that you had a pleasant trip from Okayama this morning? I'm afraid that it's terribly hot today, though. May I offer you some cold refreshment, perhaps?"

"That's very kind of you."

They sat down and the receptionist returned with two glasses of iced barley tea. Morimoto settled back into his comfortable, soft chair, and he was very grateful for the cold drink. Mr. Watanabe cleared his throat.

"As I said to you on the telephone yesterday, Inspector, we'll do everything that we can to help you with your investigation, and I do hope that it's nothing serious. We wouldn't want our hotel to be in the newspapers, involved in a big scandal!"

Mr. Watanabe laughed nervously.

"Oh, don't worry. It's nothing like that," Morimoto reassured him. "And I'm very grateful for your assistance and for taking the time to meet me today. I apologize for having given you such short notice. I hope that it's not been too inconvenient for you."

"Not at all, not at all. After receiving your telephone call yesterday afternoon, I've made some investigations along the lines that you requested concerning Mr. Ishihara's visits to our hotel. As I'm sure you'll understand, Inspector, we're generally not in the habit of discussing any matters concerning our guests. Not at all, in fact. But, of course, since this is an important police matter, as you've indicated, we'll do whatever we can to assist you. And I do hope that the information I've been able to gather will be helpful for you."

"Thank you, Mr. Watanabe. As I said, I'm very sorry to have to bother you in this way. I really hope that I haven't caused you too much trouble."

"No, really. We're only too pleased to be able to do our civic duty and assist the police with their inquiries!"

Mr. Watanabe opened up a folder that was lying on the top of his desk.

"Now, in answer to some of the questions which you asked over the telephone yesterday. I've had all of our records checked, and they confirm that Mr. Ishihara has being staying at our hotel quite regularly. To be specific, he's usually stayed here about once every month. Sometimes he'll visit twice a month, though."

Mr. Watanabe sipped his iced barley tea as he leafed through the folder.

"In fact, Inspector, I think that it's quite fair to say that Mr. Ishihara is one of our very best customers. It goes without saying that we're very grateful for that. Somebody from his office in Okayama usually calls a week or so before his visit to make his reservation. He's been staying here for the past three years. He usually stays just one or two nights, but I've noticed from the records that he has stayed longer on several occasions."

Morimoto was watching Mr. Watanabe. He nodded slowly and he drank his iced barley tea as Mr. Watanabe relayed the information from the folder.

"Have you ever met Mr. Ishihara yourself?" Morimoto asked.

"Err…well, no…I don't believe so. Not personally myself. But many of our receptionists seem to know him. At least, many of them recognize him, anyway, so I'm told."

"Yes, I see. And also, I was wondering…how does Mr. Ishihara usually pay his bill?"

"Yes, that's right, you asked me about that on the telephone yesterday. Well apparently, Mr. Ishihara always uses a credit card. As a matter of fact, it's been the same credit card every time that he's stayed here for the past three years. It's actually a company credit card, I believe, from National Electronics."

"I see. And the last time that Mr. Ishihara stayed here would have been his visit two weeks ago, wouldn't it?"

"Yes, I've checked into that. It was exactly two weeks ago. He checked in on the Wednesday evening, and he stayed for two nights. He checked out of the hotel on Friday morning."

"I was wondering then, perhaps you'd be so kind as to let me have copies of his hotel registration card for that last stay? And also, perhaps you could let me have a copy of his bill and his credit card receipt?"

"Yes, certainly Inspector, that's no problem. I can do that. I'll do that right away for you, if you'd like. Wait here just a moment, please."

Mr. Watanabe got up from behind his desk and walked out of the office.

Morimoto finished up his iced barley tea as he waited. Mr. Watanabe soon returned and handed Morimoto three sheets of photocopied paper. The first sheet was a copy of Mr. Ishihara's hotel registration card. It was the kind of registration card that everybody had to fill out when they checked into a hotel. It contained Mr. Ishihara's name and his business address, and it also showed his check in time, which was recorded as having been 9:25 on that Wednesday evening.

The second sheet of paper was Mr. Ishihara's bill, which had been given to him as he checked out of the hotel on the Friday morning. The check out time was recorded as 8:30 that morning. The third and final sheet of paper was a photocopy of the receipt from Mr. Ishihara's credit card. All three of the photocopies that Mr. Watanabe had given Morimoto had Mr. Ishihara's signature on them.

Morimoto opened his briefcase and took out a clear plastic folder into which he carefully placed the three sheets of paper. Then he put the folder back inside his briefcase and closed it up again.

"Thank you, Mr. Watanabe. Thank you very much indeed. That's very helpful."

Mr. Watanabe smiled, and he nodded his head in response.

"And also," Morimoto continued, "I wonder whether you were able to find out about the receptionists? Did you manage to find out who they were during Mr. Ishihara's last visit?"

"Oh, yes, Inspector, they're waiting to meet you. You mentioned yesterday that you wanted to meet the receptionists who'd been working on the Thursday night of Mr. Ishihara's last visit. I was able to find out which ones they were. There were two of them. From what they told me, they remember Mr. Ishihara quite well. Anyway, as I said, they're waiting to meet you if you like?"

Morimoto was glad to hear this.

"Splendid! I'd very much like to meet them if it's not too much trouble. I hope that they haven't been waiting too long?"

"Oh, that's no problem. I'll go and get them right now."

Mr. Watanabe got up from his desk again and hurried out of his office. He returned with two receptionists dressed in the same smart blue uniforms that Morimoto had seen in the lobby. They were a young man and a young lady who both looked to Morimoto to be in their middle twenties. They sat down next to Morimoto.

"I'm really so sorry to have to trouble you like this," Morimoto apologized to them. "However, I believe that you know Mr. Ishihara, don't you? Mr. Ishihara from National Electronics in Okayama?"

The receptionists both nodded.

"From what I've been told, he's a frequent visitor here, isn't he?" Morimoto continued.

"Yes, that's right," the young lady replied. "We see Mr. Ishihara quite often. He's quite a regular customer—one of the customers that we recognize, at least."

"Well then, I wanted to ask you a few questions about the last time that Mr. Ishihara stayed here. It was two weeks ago. I'm particularly interested in the Thursday evening, exactly two weeks ago today. Mr. Watanabe has told me that you were both working at the reception desk that evening, isn't that right? Do you remember that evening?"

The two young receptionists both nodded again.

"Yes," the young lady replied. "Mr. Watanabe told us that you were interested in that particular evening, and we've both been thinking about it. We can both remember talking to Mr. Ishihara on two separate occasions during that evening."

"Really?" Morimoto said. "Did Mr. Ishihara often talk to you when he stayed here, then?"

"Well, not really, but we do have a few words with him sometimes, since we recognize him, you see. And since he's quite a frequent visitor I guess that he knows us too. I guess that he recognizes us. He always seems rather talkative, and he likes to have a little chat when he's checking in and checking out, or even when he's just passing through the lobby."

The young man nodded.

"When did you first see him that evening then?" Morimoto asked.

"Well," the young lady replied, "the first time was when he returned to the hotel in the late afternoon—when he came back to the hotel after finishing his work, I guess. We both remember that he stopped at the reception desk and asked us about the baseball game that evening in the Osaka Dome."

"Can you remember about what time that would have been?" Mr. Watanabe interjected, looking thoughtful and trying to be helpful. "About what time was it that Mr. Ishihara came back to the hotel? Do you remember?"

"Well," the young lady said, "I don't think that we can remember exactly."

She looked at her colleague.

"But we know roughly when it was. It would certainly have been some time before six o'clock. That's because the baseball game started at six o'clock, you see.

We remember that Mr. Ishihara was in a very good mood, and he told us that he was rather pleased that he'd been able to finish his work so early that afternoon. He was pleased because it meant that he was able to go to the baseball game that evening. We remember that he explained to us that he'd always been a big baseball fan, but that he was usually so busy with his work that he almost never had the chance to go to a game."

The young man nodded.

"He seemed very excited at the prospect of the game that evening," the young lady continued. "Anyway, he asked us to call a taxi to take him to the Osaka Dome and he went up to his room. I suppose that it was to change his clothes or to shower or something, and he came back down about fifteen minutes later. We'd been able to get a taxi for him. It was waiting in the street just outside the hotel."

"Yes," the young man added, "I'm pretty sure that Mr. Ishihara must have come back to the hotel just before five thirty that evening. That's because I remember that he was quite pleased that he was going to be able to get to the Osaka Dome in time for the start of the baseball game at six o'clock."

Morimoto looked over at Mr. Watanabe.

"And I suppose that a taxi from here to the Osaka Dome at that time of the evening wouldn't take too long, would it?"

"Oh, no, Inspector," Mr. Watanabe replied. "The Crystal House Hotel is very well located, you know. We're very proud of that. Even during the evening rush hour it wouldn't take more than about fifteen minutes at most, I'd say."

"I see."

Morimoto looked back at the receptionists.

"And when was the other time that you saw Mr. Ishihara that evening?"

"Well," the young lady said, "that was when Mr. Ishihara came back after the baseball game. He came back to the hotel by taxi, I think, and he came over to the reception desk to talk to us. We weren't very busy at that time of the evening."

"That's right," the young man confirmed. "Mr. Ishihara was all smiling and happy because the Buffaloes had won, and he told us all about the game."

"Yes, he did," the young lady said. "He told us that the scores were tied after nine innings, so they had to play some additional innings. I remember he told us that it was a very exciting game."

"Yes," the young man added, "He told us all about the grand slam home run, didn't he? He told us that there'd been a grand slam hit by one of the Buffalo players."

"Yes, that's right. He was particularly excited about the grand slam. He told us that he'd had a great view of it. He even showed us his ticket."

Morimoto looked interested.

"Mr. Ishihara showed you his ticket, did you say? You mean his ticket stub from the game?"

"Yes, the ticket stub," said the young lady.

The young man nodded.

Morimoto considered this information for a moment and rubbed his chin before asking another question.

"Do you remember what time it was when Mr. Ishihara came back after the game?"

"Well," said the young lady, "it must have been quite late, I guess, because the game did go into extra innings. And I remember that Mr. Ishihara told us that he'd stayed right until the end of the game."

"I think that it was some time after eleven o'clock," the young man said. "Perhaps around eleven fifteen, or thereabouts."

"How long did Mr. Ishihara chat with you when he came back? Do you remember?" Morimoto asked.

"Oh, it would only have been for a few minutes, I guess," the young lady replied. "Not for very long, really. It was quite late and he must have been rather tired."

"And after talking with you, did he go up to his room right away?"

"Err...yes. That's right. He went up in the elevator, as I recall," she said.

The young man nodded.

Morimoto paused again for a few moments.

"Well, thank you both very much. That's been extremely helpful. I don't think that I have any other questions for you now."

The receptionists stood up and left the office. Mr. Watanabe looked very satisfied.

"Two fine young people, don't you think, Inspector? They do such a wonderful job at the reception desk. We're very proud of the training and efficiency of all of our staff, but we're particularly pleased with the young people who handle the front desk. They always earn the highest marks in our customer satisfaction surveys. Perhaps that's why Mr. Ishihara kept coming back here. Anyway, I hope that the information they provided was useful for your investigation. They were able to remember quite a lot about Mr. Ishihara's last visit, don't you think so?"

"Yes, they were very helpful. I'm glad that I came here today. And I think that I've taken up far too much of your time, Mr. Watanabe. I'm sure that you've many other important things to be getting on with."

Morimoto rose from his chair and picked up his briefcase. Mr. Watanabe seemed pleased that Morimoto's visit was over, and his expression also betrayed more than a little relief.

"I'll show you out, Inspector."

Mr. Watanabe hurried out from behind his desk and led Morimoto back towards the lobby. In the hallway Mr. Watanabe lowered his voice and gave Morimoto a conspiratorial glance.

"And by the way, Inspector, please let me assure you that you can depend on us to be quite discreet about your enquiries. I've given the hotel staff strict orders not to discuss your visit with anybody. In any case, it might not be very good for business if word gets around that we've been visited by a police inspector!"

Mr. Watanabe laughed nervously.

"And I suppose that Mr. Ishihara will continue to stay with us, won't he, Inspector? I don't suppose that there's any reason to believe that he won't be back, is there? We wouldn't want to lose such a valuable customer."

"Oh, don't worry, Mr. Watanabe," Morimoto said in a reassuring manner. "I'm sure that Mr. Ishihara will continue to be one of your best customers long into the future."

Mr. Watanabe was visibly pleased to hear this. They returned to the shiny, marble floor of the hotel lobby, and just as Mr. Watanabe was getting ready to say good-bye, Morimoto asked one last question.

"Ah, yes, Mr. Watanabe, I wanted to ask you one other thing. Did Mr. Ishihara, by any chance, leave anything behind in his room when he checked out after his last visit? Was there anything that he forgot to take with him?"

Mr. Watanabe looked surprised.

"Well, if there had been anything important I'm sure that we'd have forwarded it to Okayama for him. We have his address after all. But if you wait a minute I can find out for you, if you like. We keep records of all of the lost property—when and where it was found, that sort of thing. Just wait here for a moment, please, and I'll go and check up on it for you."

"That's very kind of you."

Mr. Watanabe returned several minutes later.

"There wasn't anything, Inspector. There was nothing found in Mr. Ishihara's room after he checked out that Friday morning. He didn't leave anything behind in his room. If he'd forgotten something, then it would certainly have been in our records. I've no doubt about that."

Morimoto thanked Mr. Watanabe again, and after they had exchanged bows Morimoto walked out of the hotel through the automatic sliding glass doors, back into the heat and noise of the busy Osaka street. Mr. Watanabe stood and watched Morimoto through the doors as he walked slowly away from the hotel.

CHAPTER 14

▼

After descending the steps from the Crystal House Hotel, Inspector Morimoto strolled back down the street towards Osaka railway station at a leisurely pace. It was now the hottest part of the day and the sun was beating down on the sidewalk. Morimoto loosened his tie.

When he returned to the pedestrian concourse outside the main building of Osaka railway station, he headed towards the sign for the Umeda subway station, where he walked down the series of stairs leading to the underground railway. He went over to the ticket machines and looked up at the overhead display indicating the fares required for traveling to the various other stations on the subway network. Morimoto located his destination on the sign, and he purchased a one-way ticket.

He used his ticket to pass through the automatic ticket gates and he walked onto the platform for southern bound trains of the Midosuji underground railway line. An electronic display above the platform indicated that the next train would arrive in three minutes, and Morimoto sat down on one of the platform benches to wait. The train arrived punctually, and Morimoto traveled four stops, passing underneath the central Osaka downtown area. He exited the train at Namba station and ascended the series of stairs to the street level.

The bustling Namba district is well known as the main theater district of Osaka, but it is also very well known for its restaurants, and this was much more on Morimoto's mind as he walked out of the subway station and into the fierce sunlight. Not far away, Morimoto found a narrow street lined on either side with restaurants, each one of which had a brightly lit window displaying very realistic plastic representations of the dishes that they had to offer.

Morimoto entered one of these restaurants, and even though it was only in the middle of the afternoon, he could see that it was about half full with a mix of businessmen and other clients. Morimoto supposed that the other customers may very well have been attracted to the restaurant for exactly the same reason that he himself had been attracted to it, which was the large sign in the window that offered half price beer in the afternoon before six o'clock.

Morimoto chose a seat in a quiet corner of the room, and he was soon served with a large mug of cold beer. The restaurant that he had chosen served a type of pancake that was a specialty of the Osaka region, and Morimoto had to cook it himself. His table was equipped in the middle with an electric powered, flat, iron griddle, which Morimoto's waitress switched on for him. She then made several trips to his table and brought him a series of bowls that she placed around the edges of the griddle. These bowls contained the various culinary ingredients that Morimoto would require for his meal.

Morimoto took off his jacket and placed it over one of the empty chairs beside his table. He then began the preparation of his meal by pouring oil onto the griddle, and he spread it around with a flat wide brush. Next, he picked up three slices of rather fatty bacon from one of his bowls with his chopsticks, and he laid them side-by-side on the griddle, and besides these he placed three strips of raw squid taken from another of his bowls. In the largest of his bowls, he had a pancake batter mixture, and to this he added a raw egg, which he rather expertly cracked open, single-handedly, on the side of the bowl. He then proceeded to vigorously mix these together with his chopsticks, and when they were well mixed he added some shredded, raw cabbage from another of his bowls.

Morimoto stretched his legs out under the table, he drank his beer, he turned over his bacon and his squid on the griddle with his chopsticks, and he stirred his batter mixture. He was enjoying his visit to Osaka.

When the bacon and the squid were nicely cooked, Morimoto placed them on the edge of the griddle, and he poured the batter mixture onto the center of the griddle. As it thickened, he prodded it around the edges with his chopsticks, and he fashioned it into a tidy circular shape. Then he leaned back in his chair again, and he sat there, beer glass in hand, watching it cook and looking around at the other customers in the restaurant.

After a carefully judged amount of time, Morimoto turned the pancake over, and he placed the bacon and the squid on the top of the newly browned upper side. After another couple of minutes, he poked the center of his pancake with his chopsticks to satisfy himself that the batter was cooked all of the way through, and then he switched off the power to the griddle. Finally, he carefully scooped the pancake onto his plate.

From a rack of spices and sauces on the edge of his table, Morimoto selected a thick dark brown sauce. It was slightly sweet, and it was made from soybean paste. He poured the dark sauce liberally over the top of his pancake. Next, he picked up a shaker, and he covered the sauce with a fine green coating of dried seaweed powder. Replacing the shaker on the rack, Morimoto finally selected a pot of dried fish flakes, which he also spread generously over the top of his pancake. Morimoto's pancake was now ready to eat, and he ordered another mug of beer to go along with it.

After he had finished his meal, Morimoto took quite a long time to drink his third mug of beer. The Osaka Dome was only about two kilometers away, and he did not want to get there too early. Eventually, when his watch showed that the time had reached five twenty, Morimoto got up from his table and put on his jacket. He picked up his briefcase and walked over to the cashier to pay his bill. Leaving the restaurant, he walked back down the street towards Namba subway station, and from there he walked westward away from the center of Namba.

The streets had become even more crowded with shoppers and workers leaving their offices, and Morimoto sauntered along with them in no particular hurry. At one of the street corners, he stepped into a convenience store. He walked over to the large refrigerator in the corner, where he examined the selection of ice creams in some detail, before finally selecting a vanilla cone with chocolates and nuts on top. Morimoto paid for the ice cream and unwrapped it from its paper cover, which he deposited in the trash can outside the store. He resumed his saunter along the street as he consumed his ice cream. He was really enjoying his trip to Osaka.

Before too long, Morimoto turned off the main street and he walked across a bridge spanning the Kizu River at the point where it joined the Shirinashi River, and then, exactly in accordance with his plan, he arrived at the Osaka Dome at just a few minutes before six o'clock. The Osaka Buffaloes were hosting a baseball game in the dome that evening, just as they had done on the Thursday evening, exactly two weeks before.

Viewed from the outside, the Osaka Dome is an impressive structure. It is a tall, circular, blue and silver colored building, which looks somewhat like a gigantic flying saucer that has landed in the middle of Osaka's crowded urban expanse. The outside walls of the dome are nine stories high, and they are painted a mixture of light blue and dark blue. From the top of these walls, the silver roof arches upwards even higher to its peak at the center of the building. A distinctive wide circular tunnel containing an amusement arcade and other entertainments wraps around the top edge of the outside wall, rising and falling eight times in a wave-like pattern, thereby giving the dome an octagonal appearance.

As Morimoto strolled around the pedestrian walkway surrounding the dome, he watched the Buffalo fans forming into lines at the ticket booths. Other fans crowded around the food stands that were selling cold beer and popular snacks such as fried octopus, grilled chicken, and squid. Suitably provisioned, they then filed inside the dome to watch the evening's game.

Morimoto, however, did not buy a ticket. He just waited outside the dome, looking at his watch and keeping track of the time. Then, at exactly ten minutes after six, he started walking away from the dome towards Taisho station, which was the nearest subway station. For the first time that day Morimoto walked fairly rapidly.

At Taisho station, Morimoto boarded a train on the Nagahori subway line, which left Taisho station at 6:18. At the fourth stop, which was Shinsaibashi station, he transferred to the Midosuji line along which he headed northwards, back towards Umeda station, retracing the journey that he had made earlier that afternoon. However, he did not get off the train at Umeda station. Instead, he stayed on board for another three stops until the train reached Shin-Osaka station.

At Shin-Osaka station, Morimoto stepped off the train and ascended the stairs from the subway station to the adjoining railway station. Inside the lobby of the railway station, Morimoto walked over to the ticket window and asked the attendant for a one-way ticket to Okayama on the next Nozomi bullet train. All of the seats on the Nozomi bullet train are reserved seats, and Morimoto's ticket indicated his carriage number together with his seat number.

Having purchased his ticket, Morimoto passed through the automatic ticket gate and rode the long elevator up to the bullet train platform, which was on the top floor of the station building. He stepped out onto the platform for the westbound trains at exactly 6:40, and he walked along the platform to the point where the signs indicated that his carriage would stop.

The Nozomi bullet train pulled into the platform at precisely 6:42, and when the train had come to a complete stop, the door to Morimoto's carriage was exactly in front of where he was standing. Morimoto waited to let some passengers step out of the train before climbing on board, and he placed his briefcase in the overhead rack before sinking into his assigned seat. The Nozomi bullet train left Shin-Osaka station exactly two minutes after it had arrived.

The train accelerated rapidly away from the station. It had already started to become dark outside, and from his window seat Morimoto looked out at the city lights of Osaka. The headlights of the cars and busses shone brightly in the twilight, and many of the office windows were lit up as the businessmen put in their all too often compulsory overtime. In the shopping plazas and restaurant alleys, the neon lights flashed out their advertisements.

After only ten minutes, the Nozomi bullet train was hurtling through a series of dark tunnels beneath the mountains on the northern side of Kobe. Except for these segments passing through the tunnels, the bullet train track is built on stilts quite high above the ground, and as the train emerged from the tunnels and raced along the elevated track, Morimoto was able to look down on the darkening rice fields and villages which lay spread out beneath him in the dusk. This was the same countryside that he had enjoyed so much as he had passed through it in the opposite direction that morning, although at that time it had been at a much more leisurely pace.

As the Nozomi bullet train sped along the track, it rocked gently from side to side, and every ten minutes or so there was a sharp swooshing sound in the carriage as another bullet train passed by on their right hand side, traveling just as quickly as they were in the opposite direction back towards Osaka. Morimoto's train sped through Himeji station without stopping, and the brightly lit platform passed by Morimoto's window in a blur. The Nozomi bullet trains did not make any stops between Osaka and Okayama.

By the time the train started to decelerate on its approach to Okayama station, it had become almost completely dark outside the carriage. Morimoto looked out at the lights of Okayama city, and he was able to see both the Hakken River and then the Asahi River as he passed over them. The bullet train track crossed over these rivers on its own bridges that were built just slightly upstream of the bridges carrying the Sanyo Main railway line that Morimoto had crossed over in the opposite direction earlier that morning.

The Nozomi bullet train arrived at the third floor of Okayama station at exactly 7:30. Stepping out onto the platform, Morimoto walked towards the downward escalator. One floor below, he surrendered his ticket as he passed through the automatic ticket gate, and he then walked down a flight of stairs that took him to the first floor of the station.

Morimoto looked at his watch. The time was 7:32.

CHAPTER 15

▼

Inspector Morimoto reached his office at police headquarters early the next morning, Friday, and when Police Officer Suzuki arrived he told her about his trip to Osaka. They discussed what they had learned from Mr. Watanabe and the receptionists at the Crystal House Hotel, and Suzuki took the copies of Mr. Ishihara's receipts from the hotel to examine.

Later in the morning after Suzuki had finished her investigations, Morimoto poured them both a cup of tea and he stretched out at his desk.

"Well, Suzuki, what do we know that might connect Mr. Ishihara with Mr. Sekikawa's murder? There's nothing concrete, really, except that Mr. Sekikawa worked under Mr. Ishihara in a division at National Electronics that is being investigated by Tokyo for selling national secrets abroad. And what reason do we have to doubt that Mr. Ishihara spent the evening of the murder watching a baseball game in Osaka? Again, nothing really."

"But," Morimoto continued, "let's consider the matter from another point of view. Is there any proof that Mr. Ishihara was not in Okayama on the night of the murder? Is it possible that Mr. Ishihara was in Okayama? Can we hypothetically construct a sequence of events whereby Mr. Ishihara did come to Okayama? A sequence of events that fits in with all of the other facts?"

Suzuki sipped her tea.

"Well, sir, I think it's clear that your trip yesterday establishes that it's quite possible that Mr. Ishihara was at the murder scene. At any rate, he could have been in Okayama while the murder was being committed. We can't rule out that possibility. By traveling here and back on the Nozomi bullet train, he could have visited Okayama in between the times when we have proof that he was in Osaka.

In other words, we don't have any proof that Mr. Ishihara wasn't in Okayama at the time of the murder."

"Yes, Suzuki, I agree. By the way, what did you find out from your investigations this morning?"

"I've checked into Mr. Ishihara's signature on the credit card receipt and the signatures on the hotel documents that you gave me—the registration card and the bill. They all appear to be quite genuine. There's nothing suspicious about any of them. The details of the credit card check out all right as well. We've no reason to doubt, therefore, that Mr. Ishihara really was in Osaka on those days."

"Furthermore," Suzuki continued, "it was also quite easy to trace the taxi that Mr. Ishihara used to travel to the Osaka Dome on Thursday night, because it was ordered for him by the hotel. I called up the taxi company that the Crystal House Hotel uses, and they were able to trace the driver who made that trip. She remembered picking somebody up from the hotel that evening, and she's quite certain that she dropped them off at the Osaka Dome. And furthermore, her records show that they reached the Osaka Dome just before six o'clock that evening."

"That's good," Morimoto said.

"Yes, sir, and moreover, we also know that Mr. Ishihara returned to his hotel that evening some time after eleven o'clock. The point is, though, what we don't have any information about is the intervening five hours. We've absolutely no indication of where Mr. Ishihara actually was between six o'clock and eleven o'clock that evening—no indication at all, other than his own account that he was in the Osaka Dome watching the baseball game."

Morimoto nodded his agreement.

"So if Mr. Ishihara did come to Okayama, how do you think that he did it, Suzuki?"

"Well, sir, let's suppose that when Mr. Ishihara was dropped off at the Osaka Dome by the taxi at about six o'clock, he bought a ticket for the game and he entered the dome. After ten minutes or so he could have left the dome—just walked out again while everybody else was still coming in. And as you demonstrated yesterday, he could have managed to be in the lobby at Okayama station by 7:32. That's only an hour and a half after the taxi dropped him off at the Osaka Dome. And, of course, he could have returned to Osaka later the same evening by the bullet train."

Morimoto loosened his tie.

"All right then, Suzuki, let's suppose that Mr. Ishihara really did come to Okayama in the way that you've outlined. Which train do you think that he'd have taken to return to Osaka that evening?"

"Well, sir, presumably Mr. Ishihara would have returned on one of the Nozomi bullet trains, since that's the fastest way possible. Let's assume, then, that he traveled from Okayama to the Shin-Osaka station by Nozomi bullet train, and that he then went straight to his hotel. The hotel receptionists told you that he arrived back at the hotel at about 11:15. Working back from that time, there are in fact several trains that he could have taken. In any case, the important thing is that it would have meant that he'd have been able to stay in Okayama until up to around ten o'clock that evening."

"Yes, I suppose so," Morimoto remarked. "That would have given Mr. Ishihara about two and a half hours in Okayama, from seven thirty until about ten o'clock. However, a relevant point here is that the baseball game went into extra innings, and on that particular evening the game didn't end until 10:45."

Suzuki nodded.

"If we're going to consider the possibility," Morimoto continued, "that Mr. Ishihara was using the baseball game as an alibi for his trip to Okayama, that he wanted to make it appear as though he was at the baseball game in Osaka as a cover for his secret trip to Okayama, then we have to realize that he wouldn't have known in advance that the game would be extended into extra innings."

"Yes, sir. Absolutely. That's quite right. If Mr. Ishihara had thought all of this out in advance, then it's reasonable to assume that he'd have planned it so that he could have been back in Osaka at about the time that the baseball game ended. He'd have wanted to time his return to the hotel so that it would appear as though he'd returned there directly from the baseball game, and so that it would appear that he'd left the baseball game as soon as it had finished, but not before it had finished. And in such a case, he wouldn't have planned on the game going into extra innings."

"The earliest time that a nine inning game would end would be about nine o'clock, wouldn't it?" Morimoto suggested.

"Yes, sir, that's about right. Most of the games finish some time between nine o'clock and 9:45, if they don't go into extra innings, that is. Therefore, let's consider the possibility that the game in the dome that evening might have finished at nine o'clock. If Mr. Ishihara had gone straight back to his hotel from the dome after a nine o'clock finish, he'd have reached his hotel at about 9:30, let's say."

"Consequently," Suzuki continued, "in order to give the impression to the receptionists at the hotel that he'd just returned from the baseball game, he'd in fact have needed to have planned to arrive back at Shin-Osaka station at just after nine o'clock. In other words, allowing for the earliest possible finish of the baseball game, Mr. Ishihara would have needed to have arranged his itinerary that evening so that he'd arrive back in Osaka at about nine o'clock."

"Therefore, sir, he'd probably have taken the Nozomi bullet train which leaves Okayama station at 8:32. It reaches Shin-Osaka station at exactly eleven minutes after nine. And that would mean, sir, that Mr. Ishihara would have had almost exactly one hour in Okayama, from 7:30 until 8:30."

Morimoto nodded again.

"Yes, I see what you mean, Suzuki. If Mr. Ishihara had been trying to establish an alibi, then that would have been the most careful way to do it. Presumably, he'd also have needed to keep track of the game somehow, wouldn't he? That's because he'd have needed to be able to judge at exactly what time he should return to his hotel. Don't you think so? Maybe he had a radio with him, with headphones or an earphone. He could have listened to the commentary of the game while he was riding the train."

"Yes, sir, probably something like that. He might also have been keeping track of the game while he was in Okayama. But by eight thirty the game would only have been in the seventh or eighth inning, I suppose. At that point, Mr. Ishihara wouldn't have known that the game would need extra innings, so he'd have had to take the Nozomi at 8:32 in order to be back in Osaka on time. Even at 8:30, he'd still have had to account for the possibility that the game could end soon after nine o'clock."

Morimoto nodded.

"And actually," Suzuki added, "since the game did go into extra innings, I suppose that Mr. Ishihara would have ended up with some extra time on his hands. He'd have discovered that he'd returned to Osaka much earlier than he'd needed to."

"Yes, that's quite right, Suzuki. He'd actually have had to have stayed somewhere, such as Shin-Osaka station or Osaka station perhaps, for quite a while, waiting for the baseball game to finish. He'd have had to wait for about an hour and a half, in fact. Incidentally, when you went to National Electronics to interview Mr. Ishihara about his trip, he told you that after the game had finished he returned to the Crystal House Hotel by taxi. And the hotel receptionist who I spoke with yesterday also said that she thought that Mr. Ishihara had returned to the hotel by taxi after the game. Do you think that's really the case?"

"Well, according to the events which we've postulated, he could have taken a taxi from the Osaka Dome back to the Crystal House Hotel. He'd have had time.

When he stepped off the Nozomi bullet train at Shin-Osaka station, he'd have known that the game hadn't finished, so he'd have had time to take the subway back to the Osaka Dome. At the Dome, he could have waited outside for the game to finish, and when it was all over he could have found a taxi to take him back to his hotel."

Suzuki rose from her desk and filled her teacup from the teapot sitting on the table in the middle of the room. She looked over at Morimoto, but he indicated that his cup was still full. Returning to her desk, Suzuki mentioned some additional points that had occurred to her.

"This hypothetical scenario demonstrates the possibility that Mr. Ishihara visited Okayama that evening in a way that had been very carefully planned out in advance. And there's another thing, sir, which may be relevant. It may be significant that the baseball game was played inside a dome. Let's suppose that Mr. Ishihara really did plan all of this out in advance. Since the baseball game was played inside a dome he wouldn't have needed to worry about the game being canceled because of the weather. As a matter of fact, quite a few of the other outdoor baseball games that evening had to be canceled because of the heavy rain. But you don't need to worry about that inside a dome."

"Yes, that's an interesting point," Morimoto agreed.

"Moreover, sir, when Mr. Ishihara eventually returned to his hotel late that evening, the receptionists told you that they recalled that he showed them his ticket stub from the game. They also told you that he talked to them about the grand slam home run that the Buffaloes hit in the fifth inning. If Mr. Ishihara did in fact do as we are surmising, then he'd have been able to keep his ticket stub with him from when he bought his ticket and entered the dome at six o'clock. Presumably, he'd also have learned about the grand slam from his radio or from whatever other means he'd been using to keep track of the game."

Morimoto leaned back in his chair and ran his fingers through his hair. He wondered whether anyone would actually have carried out anything remotely along the lines they had just laid out. It certainly would have required some meticulous planning, and all for the purpose of being able to spend one hour in Okayama, an hour that Mr. Ishihara would later be able to claim to have spent watching a baseball game in Osaka.

If that was really what had happened, Morimoto thought, then there must have been a very important reason for Mr. Ishihara to want to spend a secret hour in Okayama. Moreover, whatever Mr. Ishihara did during the one hour that he spent in Okayama would surely have been very carefully planned out in advance as well.

Morimoto looked over at Suzuki again.

"So if that's the case, Suzuki, Mr. Ishihara would have arrived in Okayama at just about 7:30, and he'd have left at about 8:30. That would have given him about an hour here, isn't that right?"

"Yes, sir, that's right. And, of course, the interesting thing about that hour is that it coincides with the information that we have from the pathologist, Dr. Ogata, regarding the time of Mr. Sekikawa's death."

"Exactly. So does that mean that Mr. Ishihara was directly involved in Mr. Sekikawa's murder? What do you suppose that Mr. Ishihara would have done here? Why all of the elaborate planning and clandestine movements for that one single hour?"

Suzuki frowned.

"Actually, sir, we don't know that Mr. Ishihara would necessarily have been alone. Maybe he met some people from the syndicates, and maybe he traveled together with them from Osaka?"

"It's possible," Morimoto agreed.

"In any case, sir, if Mr. Ishihara really did travel to Okayama in the manner in which we've hypothesized, then I imagine that it's quite likely that he'd have had some arrangement to meet with Mr. Sekikawa. Perhaps Mr. Sekikawa met him at Okayama station. Perhaps Mr. Ishihara's visit to Okayama that evening had something to do with the possible switching of the coin locker keys. Who knows?"

"Yes, there's still the matter of the coin locker key," Morimoto murmured.

"But regardless of the key, sir, if Mr. Ishihara was traveling with company, with a member of the syndicates, perhaps, then that might tie in to some extent with what Ms. Sakai told us. The last time that we spoke with her she told us that Mr. Sekikawa had an appointment to meet the syndicates that evening."

"Yes, that's right. What time was it that Ms. Sakai told us that she was supposed to meet Mr. Sekikawa at the station?"

"She told us that he'd asked her to meet him there at 6:30 that evening, and she said that she was supposed to bring her money with her. And she also said that when he didn't turn up she'd waited until after 7:30."

"If we're right about Mr. Ishihara, Suzuki, then there seems to have been quite a lot of people converging on Okayama station that evening. First of all there was Ms. Sakai, who claims that she had an appointment to meet Mr. Sekikawa. And next there was Mr. Ishihara arriving from Osaka, possibly accompanied by a host of syndicate members. And it all ended up with one dead body, that of Mr. Sekikawa."

They sipped their tea for a while in silence, and then Suzuki made another comment.

"If Mr. Ishihara was in Okayama that evening, as we've suggested, and if the murder did in fact take place in the alley while Mr. Ishihara was present, then that would imply that the time of the killing would have had to be very close to eight o'clock. Funnily enough, sir, that was about the time that the grand slam home run was hit in the Osaka Dome."

"Hmmm…that's true," Morimoto murmured. "A grand slam in the Osaka Dome—a lifeless body being rained upon in Okayama. The question is, where was Mr. Ishihara? Was he watching the grand slam, or was he watching the murder?"

Morimoto scratched his head and thought. He was deliberating about what he should do next. He knew that he needed to talk to Ms. Sakai again. Furthermore, he was increasingly beginning to feel that he would also like to talk to Mr. Ishihara again. Who should he talk to first, Ms. Sakai or Mr. Ishihara?

As it turned out, other developments decided the matter for him, developments that were to take place later that evening on the other side of Okayama station from where Morimoto and Suzuki were sitting that morning. It would turn out that one of the two people whom Morimoto wished to interview would voluntarily call the police headquarters and request a meeting with him. The other one would never speak to Morimoto again.

CHAPTER 16

▼

Inspector Morimoto enjoyed a pleasant dinner that evening, Friday, at home with his wife, and after complimenting her on the meal he settled into his favorite armchair with a book. However, his reading was interrupted at five minutes after nine when a phone call came through from Sergeant Yamada, and immediately afterwards a police car arrived to pick him up.

It was quite dark as Morimoto was driven through Okayama city. Just after passing Okayama station, the police car drove by the Okayama Central Hospital and pulled into the headquarters of National Electronics. Parked outside the building were an ambulance and several other police cars.

There were also several groups of policemen standing outside the building talking together, and as Morimoto climbed out of the police car, Sergeant Yamada broke away from one of the groups and walked over to meet him.

"Good evening, sir. Mr. Ishihara's office is on the sixth floor. I'll take you up there. The Chief's already there, and Mr. Nishi as well."

Morimoto followed Sergeant Yamada through the front door of the building and into the elevator. There was quite a bustle of activity throughout the sixth floor when they reached it, and Mr. Ishihara's office was particularly crowded. It was being searched by several people who Morimoto did not know, but Morimoto did know the Chief and Mr. Nishi who were talking together in one corner, and more importantly, Morimoto did recognize the body hanging by his necktie from the ceiling fan. It was Mr. Ishihara.

Morimoto thought back to his visit with the manager of the Crystal House Hotel in Osaka the previous day.

"Hmmm…Mr. Watanabe's not going to be very happy about this. He's just lost one of his best customers," he muttered to himself.

The Chief spotted Morimoto and walked over to him.

"Ah, good evening, Morimoto. I thought that you'd better come and see this. There's nothing for you to do, though. Mr. Nishi has everything under control. This is Mr. Nishi's team from Tokyo, Special Branch. Shocking, isn't it? Who'd have thought it? A clear case of suicide, there's no doubt about that. Let's have a chat tomorrow morning at headquarters, shall we? We'll fill you in on all of the details then. It looks like Mr. Nishi's investigation is over now."

As they were talking, Mr. Ishihara's body was lowered from the ceiling and placed on a trolley. Morimoto and the Chief watched as it was wheeled passed them out of the room.

"I don't expect that there's anything that will interest you here, Morimoto," the Chief continued, "but have a look around if you like. Anyhow, make sure that you stay out of the way of Special Branch, please. This is Mr. Nishi's show. He's in charge of things here."

Morimoto looked around the office. He could see that Mr. Nishi's Special Branch team was looking through Mr. Ishihara's papers very carefully. However, in the corner of the room, Morimoto spotted something that he found much more interesting. He walked over and retrieved an umbrella from the umbrella stand. It was a dark red umbrella, and Morimoto recognized it as the umbrella that Mr. Ishihara had brought with him to the police headquarters when they had met on the day after Mr. Sekikawa's murder.

Morimoto walked over to the Chief who had resumed his conversation with Mr. Nishi.

"Excuse me, sir. I'm sorry to interrupt, but I was wondering whether I might take this umbrella?"

Morimoto looked at Mr. Nishi.

"Assuming that it's of no interest to Special Branch, that is."

Mr. Nishi smiled, and the Chief looked embarrassed. Morimoto could tell that the Chief did not think that he was doing very much to impress Mr. Nishi with the competence and efficiency of the local Okayama police force, an impression that the Chief had been working so hard to cultivate over the past few months.

"Well, Morimoto," the Chief said, "Mr. Ishihara's umbrella, is it? If it's of some help to you, I don't suppose that Mr. Nishi would mind."

The Chief looked at Mr. Nishi.

"Would that be all right?" he asked.

Mr. Nishi nodded.

Before he left, Morimoto watched Mr. Nishi and his team from Special Branch for a short while as they painstakingly went through the contents of Mr. Ishihara's office. It was quite apparent to Morimoto that they were searching for something.

The next morning, Saturday, Morimoto and Police Officer Suzuki were sitting together in their office reading the newspapers. There was a pile of the morning's local and national newspapers on the table in the middle of the office, and lying next to them was Mr. Ishihara's dark red umbrella that Morimoto had obtained during his visit to National Electronics the previous evening. The Okayama Tribune had Mr. Ishihara's photograph on the front page under the banner headline "Local Businessman Found Hanged in Office."

"It seems as though Mr. Nishi has been able to keep his investigation out of the papers," Morimoto remarked.

"Yes, sir. Most of the articles seem to concentrate on the details of Mr. Ishihara's career, but they do report that National Electronics had some secret research contracts. And one paper does mention that National Electronics has recently been going through some very difficult times financially. They've also hinted at a recent scandal at the company, although no specific details are provided. Anyhow, all of the papers say that it's being treated as a suicide case."

There was a sharp knock on the door and Sergeant Yamada strode into the office, looking his normal energetic self in spite of having been up most of the night at the National Electronics building.

"Good morning, Inspector. The Chief just called. He wants to know if you can go up to see him now. He says that he wants to fill you in on last night."

As Morimoto rode the elevator up to the Chief's office on the seventh floor, he wondered what kind of a mood the Chief would be in that morning. About twenty-four hundred years ago, the Greek philosopher Plato put forward the view that government should be conducted by a select group of philosopher-rulers, who should be the most highly educated members of the society, and who would reluctantly agree to run the country even though they would much rather be left to themselves to continue their own academic pursuits. Morimoto was well aware that when it came to running the police department in Okayama city, the reality did not nearly match up to Plato's ideals of governance. Nevertheless,

Morimoto felt that the Chief was a good man, and he had always managed to get on well with him.

When Morimoto was shown into the Chief's office, he was not very surprised to find that Mr. Nishi was already there. From their haggard appearances Morimoto guessed that they had both been up all night. Morimoto sat down in front of the Chief's desk.

The Chief rubbed his eyes and looked across at Morimoto.

"Good news, Morimoto! Mr. Nishi's pretty much cleared the whole thing up. It's a straightforward case of suicide, just like I told you last night. There doesn't seem to be anything at all suspicious about it. It was Mr. Ishihara, you see. He'd been leaking the secret research. He was the one who stole the two computer chips. Mr. Nishi had been able to narrow his investigation down to Mr. Ishihara some time ago. The net was closing in on him. Very fine work, I'll say. Mr. Ishihara knew that he'd been found out. He knew that he was on the verge of being arrested."

The Chief looked over at Mr. Nishi and smiled his appreciation. Mr. Nishi nodded in response.

"We've received the post mortem report from Dr. Ogata," the Chief continued. "The death was at about eight o'clock last night, by hanging—not that there was ever much doubt about that. Mr. Ishihara was working late in his office. His secretary had gone home, but there were still some other people in the building. They said that Mr. Ishihara had gone into his office at about seven thirty, and one of them found him hanging there just after eight o'clock. It's a terrible business really, isn't it?"

Morimoto nodded.

"Anyway," the Chief said, "Mr. Nishi's Special Branch team has been through everything in Mr. Ishihara's office. You saw them there last night. I was with them. We went through his house last night as well. Terrible shock for his family, I can tell you! What we found was very incriminating. We found a great deal of evidence, just as we'd expected."

"But anyhow," the Chief continued, "as I told you, the good news is that Mr. Nishi's investigation is almost over now. He's wrapping it all up. But we're going to do our very best to keep that side of it out of the papers…national security, you know. We don't want a scandal of any kind. We're doing all right so far."

The Chief motioned towards a pile of newspapers on his desk, and smiled at Mr. Nishi again. As before, Mr. Nishi nodded. Morimoto noticed that Mr. Nishi never said anything when Morimoto was there. Perhaps it was part of his training he wondered?

"Anyway, Morimoto," the Chief added, "I wanted to let you know how things stand. And by the way, I believe that you've been doing some investigating of Mr. Ishihara yourself, haven't you? You were in Osaka the day before yesterday, isn't that right?"

"Yes, that's right, sir," Morimoto replied. "We're still working on the murder of Mr. Sekikawa. We've been trying to establish where Mr. Ishihara was at the time of the murder. He claims to have been at a baseball game in Osaka, sir, but as far as we've been able to establish, he could have been at the murder scene."

"Could he, indeed!" said the Chief. "Well, you won't be able to ask him about that now, will you! That's one thing that's certain. Anyway, Mr. Nishi and I know quite a lot about Mr. Sekikawa. He was under suspicion for some time regarding the leaks. For a while, it really looked as though he might be the culprit, didn't it, Mr. Nishi?"

Mr. Nishi nodded again.

"That's why we were quite concerned about his murder, Morimoto. For a while we thought that it might have been related to our investigation. It turns out, though, that we were barking up completely the wrong tree there. It was Mr. Ishihara who we were after."

"Do you mean to say that Mr. Sekikawa wasn't involved in the leaking at all?" Morimoto asked. "Could he have been leaking the company secrets together with Mr. Ishihara, perhaps?"

"No, no, Morimoto. It was a one-man job, we're certain of that now. We're sure that Mr. Sekikawa didn't have anything to do with it at all. We've sorted the whole matter out, haven't we, Mr. Nishi?"

Mr. Nishi nodded.

"That's interesting," Morimoto said.

"Yes," the Chief continued. "But as I said, at the time that Mr. Sekikawa was murdered, we rather thought that it might have had something to do with Mr. Nishi's investigation. That's why I had you up here to meet Mr. Nishi. But apparently, it seems to have been an unrelated incident. So this will clarify some aspects of your investigation into Mr. Sekikawa's murder, won't it? You told me that Mr. Sekikawa was in considerable debt to the syndicates, didn't you? Surely it's clear now that it was the syndicates who killed Mr. Sekikawa because of his money problems?"

"We've no evidence to the contrary," Morimoto admitted, "although there are still some rather puzzling aspects to the case. For example, as I mentioned before, there's the curious incident of the contents of the coin locker."

The Chief looked surprised.

"But you told me that there wasn't anything in the coin locker," he said.

"Exactly, sir," Morimoto replied. "That's what's so curious."

The Chief scratched his head. This seemed to remind him of something, but he could not quite place it. Mr. Nishi looked completely blank. There was a pause in the conversation.

"By the way, Morimoto," the Chief said, eventually, "do you have any evidence linking Mr. Ishihara to the incident at all? I mean, is there anything that links Mr. Ishihara to Mr. Sekikawa's murder?"

"No, sir, actually there isn't," Morimoto said. "We don't have any concrete evidence linking Mr. Ishihara to the murder case. But as a matter of fact, I'd been planning to interview him again. There were a couple of points that I'd wanted to check up on."

"Well, Morimoto, as I told you, you're too late for that now! And as far as we're concerned, Mr. Ishihara is not going to cause us any more trouble. It's been a thoroughly bad set of events, though, hasn't it? Bad for that company, and bad for Okayama, I'll say. That man was a thief, stealing from National Electronics. And more than that, he was a traitor, selling out his country. Why, he could have hurt our whole electronics industry for the next ten years! Quite unthinkable really, a man in his position, and with his abilities. You can't be a fool to reach a position like his in that company, you know. He had a head on his shoulders for sure. Such a waste of talent!"

The Chief seemed to be indicating that the meeting was over, but Morimoto sat and thought for a few moments. Then he asked the Chief a question.

"If you don't mind, sir, there's something that I've been wondering about. Perhaps you'd be able to tell me how long Mr. Ishihara had been under investigation concerning the leaks? Or more exactly, how long is it since Mr. Ishihara would have known that an investigation was under way at all, and when would he have known that he'd become the main target of suspicion?"

The Chief looked at Mr. Nishi.

"Well, you know, Morimoto," he said, "it's been a couple of months at least that Mr. Nishi's been working on this. And the net has been tightening around Mr. Ishihara for a good four or five weeks now. And I'm sure that Mr. Ishihara must have known for at least a month or so that he could be under suspicion. That's at least a month before he decided to kill himself. Wouldn't you agree, Mr. Nishi?"

Mr. Nishi nodded.

"I see," said Morimoto, thoughtfully. "So that would mean that at the time of Mr. Sekikawa's murder, Mr. Ishihara already knew about Mr. Nishi's investigation, or at least the possibility that such an investigation was taking place. And he'd have known that he was a potential target of the investigation, wouldn't he?"

The Chief yawned and covered his mouth with his hand.

"Yes, Morimoto, I think it's fair to assume that Mr. Ishihara would have known that something was up by then. Mr. Sekikawa's murder was only about two weeks ago, wasn't it?"

"Yes, sir, that's right."

Morimoto reflected on what the Chief had told him.

"Was there a lot of money involved, sir? I suppose that when Mr. Ishihara sold the secrets—sold the first computer chip—he'd have received quite a large amount of money, wouldn't he? You did say that a payment was made on the first computer chip, the one that was recovered overseas, and that the payment had been traced to the syndicates. Presumably, Mr. Ishihara must have received some of the payment. Have you found any of the money?"

The Chief smiled.

"Yes, that's right, Morimoto. It seems that Mr. Ishihara had some contacts in the syndicates who helped him sell the first chip. He did receive a lot of money for the leaks, and we've found it all. Actually, I was there myself when it was discovered. It was late last night at Mr. Ishihara's home. As I told you, after we searched his office we also went and searched his house. We found the money there."

"Was it a lot of money, sir?"

"Oh, yes, Morimoto, it was a small fortune. It was in large denomination notes, packed inside a money belt. You know, the kind of money belt that you can wear around your waist, inside your shirt so that nobody will notice it. Easy to hide."

"I see, sir. Well then, that must have been what Special Branch were looking for last night in Mr. Ishihara's office?"

"That's right, Morimoto. We were certainly looking for the money."

Morimoto looked at Mr. Nishi.

"Well, congratulations, Mr. Nishi. It seems that your investigation has gone very well indeed."

Mr. Nishi smiled.

"By the way," Morimoto continued, "did you manage to find everything that you were searching for last night in Mr. Ishihara's office and home?"

Mr. Nishi looked uncomfortable, and there was an awkward silence for a moment before the Chief spoke up.

"Now, now, Morimoto. You know Mr. Nishi's investigation is very sensitive and he can't be discussing all of the details with the whole Okayama Police Department, can he? As I said, Mr. Nishi's work is almost done here, and it's a very fine job that Special Branch has done. We should all be very grateful to them."

C H A P T E R   17

▼

Inspector Morimoto returned to his office and told Police Officer Suzuki what he had learned from his meeting with the Chief.

"The Chief's right, sir," Suzuki said. "It does simplify our investigation into Mr. Sekikawa's murder. If Special Branch are certain that Mr. Sekikawa had nothing to do with the leaks from National Electronics, then that eliminates a lot of possibilities concerning the murder. It certainly makes it more probable that the murder was carried out by the syndicates because of Mr. Sekikawa's debts."

"Yes, Suzuki, you're right. Still, I can't help feeling disappointed that we won't be able to talk to Mr. Ishihara again. I'd rather like to have been able to question him a little more deeply about that exciting baseball game that he claimed to have watched on the evening of Mr. Sekikawa's murder. I remember how enthusiastic he sounded about it when I met him."

However, as Morimoto and Suzuki contemplated their inability to obtain any further information from Mr. Ishihara, the next development in the murder case was already under way. It was a quite unexpected development, and one that would actually reveal a great deal about the activities of Mr. Ishihara on that Thursday evening—far more, in fact, than Mr. Ishihara himself would likely have divulged.

It started with Sergeant Yamada entering the office.

"The reception desk has received a call from Ms. Sakai, sir. She's asking to speak to you. Shall I put the call through to your desk?"

Morimoto and Suzuki looked at each other. Ms. Sakai was the other person who they had wanted to interview again.

"Yes, Sergeant," Morimoto said. "Put her through to my desk, please."

Morimoto picked up his phone and waited for the line to be connected.

"Good morning, this is Inspector Morimoto."

Ms. Sakai's voice on the other end of the line was a little nervous, a little unsure.

"Good morning, Inspector Morimoto. I hope that I'm not bothering you, but I'd really like to talk with you again. Could I perhaps come over to the police station to meet you? Would that be all right?"

"Yes, of course it would be all right. Where are you now, Ms. Sakai? Would you like me to send a car for you? It wouldn't be any trouble."

"No…no…it's all right, I don't need a car. I'm at my apartment now. I'll come by myself to the police station. Is it all right if I come right away?"

"Yes, of course. I'll be waiting for you."

Morimoto hung up the phone.

"Well, Suzuki, a new development. Ms. Sakai has something that she'd like to tell us."

Suzuki's eyebrows moved marginally higher.

"I see, sir. That is an interesting development."

"Yes, and I rather feel that this time she's going to have yet another account of what happened on the night of the murder—a different account from the two that she's already given us."

"Yes, that wouldn't surprise me either, sir. But I think that we can realistically hope that this time her account will be much closer to the truth."

"Yes, I think that you're right, Suzuki."

It did not take Ms. Sakai very long to reach the police headquarters on that Saturday morning. The reception desk at the entrance to the building had been notified that she would be coming. When she arrived just after eleven o' clock she was escorted directly to one of the interview rooms on the second floor, where she was soon joined by Morimoto and Suzuki. It was the same interview room that Morimoto had used for his meeting with Mr. Ishihara on the day after Mr. Sekikawa's murder.

Ms. Sakai stood up when Morimoto and Suzuki entered the room, and they all politely exchanged bows. They sat down around the rectangular wooden table placed in the center of the interview room, with Ms. Sakai seated in the middle of one of the long sides of the table, and with Morimoto seated opposite her. Suzuki sat at the short end of the table, to Morimoto's left and on Ms. Sakai's right hand side.

As they looked at her, Morimoto and Suzuki could see that Ms. Sakai appeared quite worried. She seemed to be somewhat more distressed than on the previous two occasions when they had talked with her, and Morimoto and Suzuki both sensed that she was going to tell them something quite important about Mr. Sekikawa's murder case.

Ms. Sakai shifted uncomfortably in her chair, and she looked over at Morimoto.

"Thank you very much for meeting me again, Inspector," she said in a soft voice. "I'm sorry to call you up so suddenly."

Morimoto smiled gently.

"That's quite all right. You're looking rather concerned today, I think. Is anything the matter? I hope that there's some way in which we can help you?"

Ms. Sakai looked down at the table.

"Yes, I am rather worried. You're quite right. I found out this morning about Mr. Ishihara's suicide. I read about it in the Okayama Tribune. His photo was on the front page. You must know all about it, of course. I know about Mr. Ishihara because he was the head of Atsushi's division at National Electronics. Seeing him in the paper like that, and his suicide…it has made me rather worried."

Ms. Sakai paused for a moment.

"Well," she continued, hesitantly, "as a matter of fact, I've really been quite worried for a while now, ever since Atsushi was killed. I've been quite scared. I don't understand what's been going on. That's why I didn't tell you all about it before. What I told you last time wasn't really everything. In fact, I'm afraid that I rather misled you."

Ms. Sakai blushed slightly. She looked up at Morimoto briefly, and then she looked back down at the table again.

"I'm afraid that there's really quite a lot of things that I didn't tell you before," she continued. "But it was because I was scared, you see. I know now that I should have told you everything. I'm really sorry that I didn't tell you everything, but it was so confusing, and I was worried that something might happen to me. Anyway, I didn't tell you what really happened on the night when Atsushi was murdered. And what I told you about the reason for withdrawing my money from the bank…well that wasn't really true either."

Ms. Sakai paused again. Morimoto looked over at Suzuki.

"That's all right, Ms. Sakai," Suzuki said, reassuringly. "Actually, we'd already guessed that you hadn't told us everything. We'd already realized that what you told us about withdrawing your money from the bank wasn't completely true. So we're glad that you've come to talk to us again."

Ms. Sakai sighed and leaned back in her chair.

"Oh, really? You knew already, did you?"

She looked embarrassed, but she also appeared to be a little relieved. Morimoto and Suzuki waited patiently for her to continue talking.

"Please take your time," Suzuki remarked after a few moments, "and please tell us everything that you know. Tell us what happened, starting from the beginning. Please tell us everything that happened."

Ms. Sakai took a deep breath.

"Well," she began again, rather quietly, "it all started on the Wednesday evening. That was our last evening together, although we didn't know it at the time. But you have to remember that we'd both been under a tremendous amount of stress for a long while, Atsushi and myself. We'd been under a great deal of pressure from the syndicates. It was because of the money that Atsushi owed them, of course. It was really difficult, you know. We couldn't live a normal life. We wanted to escape somehow, we wanted to escape together."

"It began with the phone call on Wednesday evening," Ms. Sakai continued. "That's when we had our idea, and that's when we made our plan. You see Mr. Ishihara had talked to Atsushi a few days beforehand. Mr. Ishihara had told Atsushi that he was going to help him…that he was going to help him with his money problems. We trusted him. It seemed to offer us a lifeline. Mr. Ishihara said that he had a business contact in Osaka from whom he could raise some money. He said that he could help Atsushi pay off a large part of his debts to the syndicates."

Morimoto and Suzuki were watching Ms. Sakai closely.

"So you see," Ms. Sakai continued, "Mr. Ishihara said that he'd arrange everything. He said that he'd get the money, and he said that he'd set up the meeting with the syndicates. Mr. Ishihara had a business trip to Osaka arranged for that week, and he told Atsushi that he'd call him from Osaka on Wednesday evening. He said that he wanted to help us because he'd known Atsushi for a long time. He said that he wanted to help get the syndicates off Atsushi's back. He said that it was the sort of thing that he'd do for anybody in his division, if he had the chance. Apparently, Mr. Ishihara had business contacts in Osaka who knew the right people in the syndicates to sort out the whole matter, at least that's what he told Atsushi."

"The thing is, though, Mr. Ishihara cautioned Atsushi not to tell anybody about it. He wanted Atsushi to keep it all a secret. But anyway, I knew about it as well—Atsushi discussed it with me. He discussed everything with me. We didn't have any secrets. And so on Wednesday night we were both waiting for Mr. Ishihara to telephone from Osaka."

Morimoto nodded slowly. Suzuki sat quite still.

"So the telephone call that came to Atsushi's apartment on that Wednesday evening was from Mr. Ishihara," Ms. Sakai said. "It wasn't from the syndicates, as I told you before. The telephone call came from Mr. Ishihara, just as we were expecting. It was a very short call. He just told Atsushi that he'd been able to get the money, and he said that he'd be able to bring it to Okayama the following evening."

Ms. Sakai shifted in her chair again.

"And Mr. Ishihara gave Atsushi some instructions," she continued. "He told Atsushi to be waiting for him at Okayama station at seven thirty the next evening. And he also told Atsushi to get the key to one of the coin lockers at Okayama station beforehand. He said that it needed to be one of the large coin lockers, the kind that is usually on the bottom row of the lockers."

"And in the telephone call, Mr. Ishihara told Atsushi that after he arrived at Okayama station, they'd put the money in the coin locker together, and then they'd go to meet the syndicates. Mr. Ishihara said that he'd arranged a meeting with them. Mr. Ishihara told Atsushi that they'd give the syndicates the key to the coin locker."

Ms. Sakai paused, and she looked around the table at Morimoto and Suzuki whose faces were quite expressionless.

"I see," said Morimoto. "Yes, I see."

"Mr. Ishihara hadn't told us anything about a coin locker before," Ms. Sakai added, "so that was a bit of a surprise for us. In the phone call, he just said to make sure that it was one of the big lockers. We guessed that those were the instructions from the syndicates."

The three of them sat in silence for a while. Then Suzuki leaned forward and looked at Ms. Sakai.

"And I suppose that was when you made your plan, was it?" Suzuki prompted. "Was that when you and Mr. Sekikawa came up with your plan?"

Ms. Sakai nodded slowly.

"Yes," she said, "you're right. That was when we came up with our plan. It was rather on the spur of the moment, I guess. Anyhow, we worked the whole thing out together on that Wednesday evening."

Ms. Sakai paused again before continuing.

"You see we'd just had enough of it all. We'd just had enough of always worrying about what the syndicates might do. The last few months had really become very difficult for us both. Our plan seemed to give us an escape route."

Suzuki nodded.

"Yes, I'm sure that we can all understand that, Ms. Sakai," she said, sympathetically. "It must have been very difficult for you and Mr. Sekikawa. You wanted to get away from it all, get away from all of the stress and worry? You wanted to escape together, isn't that right?"

Ms. Sakai looked at Suzuki.

"Yes, that's exactly right," she agreed. "You see, even if we'd given the syndicates Mr. Ishihara's money, we'd still have owed them some more money. And we'd still have had to pay back Mr. Ishihara, somehow, as well. We discussed it, the two of us, and we realized that it wouldn't really have left us in a much better position. And there was something about Mr. Ishihara as well. To be totally honest with you, Atsushi said that he never really liked him that much, and we weren't sure whether we could completely trust him. We weren't sure what his motive really was for getting involved. We were worried that we might end up in an even worse position than before. Who knows?"

Suzuki nodded. Ms. Sakai paused and looked down at the table again. She seemed to find it difficult to continue, so Suzuki decided to help her.

"You were going to try to take the money yourselves, weren't you? The money that Mr. Ishihara was bringing from Osaka? You were going to run away with it together, weren't you?"

Ms. Sakai sighed.

"Yes," she admitted, "you're quite right. That was our plan. That was what we decided to do that Wednesday evening. That was the plan that we made after we'd received the call from Mr. Ishihara. We just wanted to run away together, to start a new life somewhere else. We were going to go abroad, actually. We thought that would be the safest thing. I don't know quite how it would have worked out, but we were going to give it a try, anyway."

"But we needed some money, you see," Ms. Sakai continued. "We needed some money to get us started, at least. So the money that Mr. Ishihara was bringing from Osaka seemed to be an opportunity for us. Atsushi argued that it was pointless to give it to the syndicates. He said that he'd still basically be in just the same position that he was in before. Anyway, Atsushi thought that if he could just get that money himself, it would be enough for us to make a fresh start somewhere together. That was what we had in mind."

Ms. Sakai stopped again.

"I understand," Suzuki said, sympathetically.

Morimoto and Suzuki were both looking intently at Ms. Sakai's face.

"And that was why you withdrew your savings from your bank on Thursday, wasn't it?" Suzuki added. "It was because you were planning to run away together, to go overseas. Am I right?"

"Yes, yes, that's right," Ms. Sakai said. "Our plan was to get the money from Mr. Ishihara on Thursday evening, and then we were going to leave the country on Friday. So I wanted to take my own savings with me as well. It wasn't much money, I know—not compared with the amount that Mr. Ishihara was supposed to be bringing to Okayama, at least. But anyway, it seemed silly to me not to take it with us."

"After we left the country," Ms. Sakai continued, "I wasn't sure that I'd be able to get a hold of my savings again. That was why I took it out from my bank on Thursday. I know that I told you before that I withdrew my savings so that Atsushi could give the money to the syndicates. But that wasn't the reason at all. I took my money out of the bank because we were planning to run away together."

"Yes, I see," Suzuki said.

There was another short period of silence in the interview room. Ms. Sakai had already explained a great deal to Morimoto and Suzuki. Nevertheless, they both realized that there was an important part of her story that still remained untold.

"Well then," Suzuki began again quietly, "what exactly was your plan? How did you and Mr. Sekikawa intend to get the money for yourselves, the money that Mr. Ishihara had said that he'd bring from Osaka?"

Ms. Sakai frowned.

"Well, we came up with the idea on Wednesday evening. It was what Mr. Ishihara had told Atsushi over the phone about the coin locker that gave us the idea. Mr. Ishihara had said that after he met Atsushi they'd put the money in the coin locker. And he'd said that he wanted Atsushi to get the key in advance. So we had this idea, you see."

Ms. Sakai looked across at Morimoto and Suzuki.

"We planned to switch the keys," she said.

CHAPTER 18

▼

Neither Inspector Morimoto nor Police Officer Suzuki registered any discernable emotion in their expression as Ms. Sakai revealed to them that she had made a plan with Mr. Sekikawa to switch the coin locker keys. They sat in silence, patiently waiting for Ms. Sakai to continue with her description of the events that had unfolded prior to Mr. Sekikawa's murder.

"So on Wednesday evening," Ms. Sakai said, "after we'd thought up our plan, Atsushi and I went out to Kurashiki station. There's a small room of coin lockers there, just off from the main station area, and we searched among the lockers to find the ones that weren't being used. And we wrote down the numbers of all of the coin lockers that weren't occupied. After that, we took the short train ride to Okayama station and we searched among the large coin lockers there as well. We were looking for a large locker that had the same number as one of the lockers that had been available at Kurashiki station."

Morimoto and Suzuki were watching Ms. Sakai closely.

"Well, in fact," Ms. Sakai continued, "there were quite a lot of numbers to choose from. Anyway, we settled on locker two hundred and three. I can still remember the number. So we paid the money into the coin locker, three hundred yen, and then we locked it and removed the key. That was locker two hundred and three at Okayama station, of course. We had obtained a key to one of the large coin lockers at Okayama station, exactly in accordance with Mr. Ishihara's instructions."

"Then we took the train back to Kurashiki, and we put three hundred yen into locker two hundred and three at that station. So you see, we were able to get that key as well. And then we had two keys, both for a coin locker with the number two hundred and three. You know, the tags on the keys are pretty much the same, and the keys looked quite similar, so actually we had to be quite careful not to get them both mixed up."

Ms. Sakai paused, and she looked at Morimoto and Suzuki before continuing with her explanation.

"Anyway, back at Atsushi's apartment that evening, we rehearsed the rest of our plan. On Thursday morning, we took the train together to Okayama just as we normally did, and Atsushi took both of the keys with him. I remember that he kept the key to the locker at Okayama station in his right pocket, and he had the key to the locker at Kurashiki station in his left pocket. Then we said goodbye to each other at Okayama station. Of course, as you know our plan didn't work, and that was the last time that we ever spoke to each other."

The sadness returned to Ms. Sakai's face, the sadness that Morimoto had noticed in her when they had met before.

"Well, anyway," Ms. Sakai continued, "the plan that we'd made was like this. Atsushi was going to wait for Mr. Ishihara at Okayama station at seven thirty, just as they'd agreed when they'd spoken on the telephone the night before. Mr. Ishihara had asked Atsushi to be waiting for him by Momotaro's statue—you know, the statue just outside the station."

Morimoto and Suzuki nodded, and Ms. Sakai continued.

"But Atsushi was going to have both of the keys with him, not just the key to the locker at Okayama station that Mr. Ishihara had asked for. And our plan was that I'd also be at the station, and I'd be watching what happened. But I was going to keep out of sight as much as possible. In any case, I'd never met Mr. Ishihara before, so we thought that there wouldn't be any danger of him recognizing me. And if there were any syndicate members with him, then we thought that they wouldn't know me either."

"Then when Mr. Ishihara arrived, we expected that they'd put the money in the locker at Okayama station, using the key that Atsushi had with him, and then we expected that they'd go off somewhere. Mr. Ishihara had said during the telephone call that after they'd put the money in the coin locker the two of them would go off together to meet the syndicates. So that was the moment when we planned that Atsushi would drop the key off for me to retrieve somehow."

"Our plan was that after the money was in the locker, Atsushi would leave the key somewhere where I could get it. He had a packet of tissues in his right pocket, which was where he had the key to the Okayama locker, and he was going to leave a tissue in a trash can somewhere, but with the key wrapped inside the tissue, or something like that. I'd be watching him, and when it was safe, when Atsushi and Mr. Ishihara had gone away, I was going to retrieve the key from the trash can so that I'd be able to take the money out of the locker."

"Our plan was that after I had the money I'd go home to my apartment in Takashima, and I was going to wait for Atsushi to come and join me there. The tricky part of the plan, or so we thought, was that Atsushi somehow had to make his escape from Mr. Ishihara and the syndicates. Atsushi would have the other coin locker key with him, which everybody else would think was the key to the locker at Okayama. So if he needed to, he could simply give that key to the syndicates. We thought, from what Mr. Ishihara had told us, that Atsushi and Mr. Ishihara would both go off somewhere else to meet the people from the syndicates, and that they'd hand over the coin locker key there. And our plan was that Atsushi would hand over the wrong key, without anybody knowing."

"Of course, we didn't know exactly how our plan would work out. We thought that maybe Mr. Ishihara might take the key from Atsushi. We really weren't sure what would happen. In any case, the plan was just that somehow, after the money had been put into the locker, Atsushi had to try to drop off the real key for me. Then Atsushi had to give me enough time to get the money out of the locker and to get safely away from the station. Then he could attempt to make his own escape from Mr. Ishihara and the syndicates, one way or another."

Ms. Sakai shrugged.

"Actually, I'd hoped that Atsushi wouldn't need to meet the people from the syndicates at all. When we made our plan on Wednesday night, I'd urged him to run away from Mr. Ishihara as soon as it was safe for him to do so. And I told him again on Thursday morning, as we were going to Okayama on the train. We were planning to leave town that evening, after he'd made his escape and reached my apartment in Takashima. We were planning to get out of Okayama as soon as possible, and we were hoping to get a flight out of Japan the next day. But Atsushi thought it would be better if he played along as much as possible, and that was really why he wanted to have the identical key. He thought that it would give me more time to get the money, and maybe allow him to get away from Mr. Ishihara and the syndicate people without arousing their suspicions."

Ms. Sakai stopped and looked at Morimoto and Suzuki. She wondered what they thought about the plan that she had made with Mr. Sekikawa.

"I know you must be thinking that it was wrong of us to try to take all of the money for ourselves and run away, and you're right, of course. Perhaps we made our decision too hastily on the Wednesday night? Perhaps it was really our own fault that Atsushi was killed?"

In fact, although he was not going to say so, at that moment Morimoto was not particularly concerned with the rights and wrongs of taking the money from Mr. Ishihara and the syndicates. Instead, he was quite impressed with the plan that Mr. Sekikawa and Ms. Sakai had concocted. He thought that it was a clever plan, although it was clearly rather dangerous, and Morimoto realized that something had obviously gone quite wrong with it. After all, Mr. Sekikawa had ended up being killed.

"Yes, I see, Ms. Sakai," Morimoto said. "I think that I can understand your plan. I can see how you'd worked the whole scheme out with Mr. Sekikawa, and now I understand why you withdrew your savings and closed your bank account on Thursday morning. But on Thursday evening your plan didn't work out as you'd expected, did it? I suppose that the actual events that evening didn't unfold in the way that you'd planned. What actually did happen? Would you be able to tell us about that now, please?"

Ms. Sakai shifted in her chair, and she took a deep breath again.

"Well," she began, "Mr. Ishihara did come to Okayama station. He arrived at just after seven thirty, as we were expecting. Atsushi was waiting for him by Momotaro's statue as they'd arranged, and I was watching them. Following our plan, Atsushi and I didn't meet each other or talk to each other that evening. We arrived at the station separately. I arrived first, and I found a seat on a bench at one of the bus stops outside the station from where I had a clear view of the statue. I saw Atsushi arrive at about 7:20 and I watched him waiting at the statue. It was raining, and he had his umbrella up."

"I can remember that I was very worried, very nervous. Anyway, when Mr. Ishihara arrived, that's when things started going wrong. They didn't go straight into the station as we were expecting. They didn't go straight to the coin locker. Instead, Mr. Ishihara took Atsushi in the other direction, away from the station entrance."

"Well, I didn't know what I should do at first. I was in a bit of a panic, but I knew that I had to keep track of where they went, so I followed them, at a distance of course. They went into the hotel next to the station. You know, the big hotel, the Grandview Hotel. And I went into the hotel as well. It has a very big lobby, as I'm sure you know, so I was able to maintain quite a distance from them. I saw that they went directly over to the elevators, and then they disappeared inside one of them. I thought that our plan had already failed. I thought that they were probably meeting the syndicates somewhere in the hotel, maybe in one of the rooms. I guessed that Mr. Ishihara had changed his mind about using the coin locker."

"But anyhow, I waited around in the hotel lobby watching to see if they'd return, and they did. They stepped out of an elevator again very soon afterwards—it was only maybe five minutes or so later. It was still just the two of them, Atsushi and Mr. Ishihara. There wasn't anybody else with them."

"And then they walked back out of the hotel, and they headed back towards the station entrance, and I followed them again. This time they went straight to the coin locker and I saw Atsushi take the key out of his pocket, the pocket on his right hand side. Atsushi opened up the locker, number two hundred and three. And then I saw them put an umbrella inside the locker, and then they closed it up again. They put three hundred yen into the slot, and they turned the key and locked it again."

"I was watching them very carefully, and I saw that Atsushi kept the key. And he put it back into his right pocket. Then the two of them started walking out of the station again, and I followed them. And Atsushi wiped his face with a tissue, and he left the tissue in one of the trash cans at the entrance as they left the station. I stayed behind in the station, of course, and I watched them leave together. That was the last time that I ever saw Atsushi."

Morimoto was gently rubbing his chin. Suzuki was sitting perfectly still. They were both staring at Ms. Sakai, absorbed in her story.

"So after they'd left the station," Ms. Sakai continued, "I went over to the trash can, and I found the tissue. And just as I'd expected, it had the key wrapped inside it. I became quite excited because it seemed to me that our plan was working after all. I took the key and went back to locker two hundred and three, and I opened it up just as we'd planned. I took the umbrella from the locker—it was rather heavy and I could tell that it had something concealed inside it. Then I went back to Takashima on the next train and went straight to my apartment. And when I was inside my apartment I opened up the umbrella."

Ms. Sakai looked at Morimoto.

"The umbrella should have had the money inside it, shouldn't it?" she said. "That's what I'd been anticipating as I'd carried it home. But it didn't have any money in it at all! It just had some documents, some plans and diagrams and things, and a little plastic box with some kind of electrical component inside. I couldn't understand what they were. But it seemed to have ruined our plan, anyway. We wanted money to run away with, but instead all that we had were these diagrams and things. Well, I didn't know what I should do, so I just waited in my apartment…and waited and waited. I was very upset, and as you know, Atsushi never came. That was when they killed him."

Ms. Sakai looked at Morimoto and Suzuki again and shrugged.

"Well," she said, "that's what happened. Now you know all of it. This time I've really told you everything."

Morimoto ran his fingers through his hair as he watched Ms. Sakai. There was no doubt in his mind that this time she really was telling the complete truth.

"What did you do with the documents?" Morimoto asked quietly. "The papers that you found in the umbrella, and the plastic box. What did you do with them?"

Ms. Sakai took a large brown envelope out of her handbag and handed it over to Morimoto.

"I've brought them for you," she replied. "As I said, I can't understand what they are, but I thought that they might be important."

Morimoto reached inside the envelope and took out the small plastic box. He opened it up. Inside was a small computer chip, just as he had expected. He closed the box and replaced it in the envelope, which he laid on the table in front of him.

"And what about the umbrella?" he asked. "The umbrella that these documents were wrapped inside. Do you still have the umbrella at your apartment?"

"The umbrella?" Ms Sakai replied. "Err…well, actually…actually I threw the umbrella into the river a few days afterwards. I was scared. I wanted to get rid of all of the links that I had with the events of that evening. I didn't want Mr. Ishihara or the syndicates to know that I'd emptied the locker. So I threw the umbrella into the Asahi River when nobody was looking. I almost threw the documents away as well, and that electrical thing, but in the end I kept them, as you can see."

Ms. Sakai seemed relieved to have finally told them the whole story.

"But," she continued, "there are quite a few things that I don't understand. For example, I can't understand why Atsushi dropped the key off for me at all. Our arrangement had been that he'd only leave me the key if the locker had the money in it. You see if there wasn't any money in the locker, our plan of running away would have had to be canceled, wouldn't it? If we didn't have the money then we couldn't run away, could we? So since the money wasn't in the locker, he shouldn't have left me the key. But he did leave me the key. That's one thing that I don't understand."

Ms. Sakai looked questioningly at Morimoto and then at Suzuki.

"Since Atsushi left the key for me, he must have wanted me to retrieve the umbrella from the locker. And that's why I was so surprised when I opened up the umbrella later on in my apartment. I was expecting to find the money in it, but all that it had was those papers and the little plastic box."

"If it didn't have the money in it, why did Atsushi drop the key off for me? Perhaps he thought that the documents were valuable. Maybe Atsushi thought that we might be able to sell the documents. I don't know. Anyway, it really doesn't matter because in the end, Atsushi wasn't able to escape from them. They killed him."

Ms. Sakai took a handkerchief from her bag and wiped her eyes. Morimoto and Suzuki waited in silence.

"And there's something else that I want to tell you," Ms. Sakai continued eventually. "Something else rather strange, something that you ought to know, I think. I saw Mr. Ishihara's photograph on the front page of the paper this morning, but it looked a bit different from the person who met Atsushi at Okayama station."

"The person who met Atsushi at the station that evening was wearing glasses, and he had a mustache. And he also had much more hair than Mr. Ishihara has in the photograph in the newspaper. It might have been the same person, though. I'm not sure. I've never actually met Mr. Ishihara, and I didn't get a very close view of the person who met Atsushi that evening. I just assumed that the person who met Atsushi was Mr. Ishihara, since that's who he was expecting."

Ms. Sakai sat back in her chair and looked over at Morimoto and Suzuki. She felt very relieved that she had finally told them everything, but she had no idea what they thought of her and Mr. Sekikawa.

"You know," Ms. Sakai added, "I feel very glad that I've told you everything at last. It's so good to get everything off my chest. These past couple of weeks since Atsushi's death have been absolutely awful. I've no idea what you think about Atsushi and myself, and as I said, I know that we did some things that we shouldn't have done."

"But you know, he wasn't a bad man at all, Atsushi. He'd got himself into some trouble, I admit, but he was really a good man. He was very kind and considerate. You could easily tell that about him when you really got to know him well. He'd made some mistakes when he was younger, it's true, but so have a lot of people. He was working hard to recover and get his life under control. And he didn't deserve to die in that way."

Ms. Sakai's voice started to tremble.

"I just wish now, more than anything else, that the people who did that to Atsushi could be caught. And I wish that they could be brought to justice!"

Ms. Sakai paused to recover her composure and she wiped her eyes again. Then she looked up at Morimoto and continued.

"I guess that you're also wondering why I decided to come here today and to tell you everything. I'd wondered whether I should tell you before, but I was worried about Mr. Ishihara and the syndicates. You see I didn't know what Atsushi might have told them before he was killed. Maybe he'd admitted dropping off the key for me? So I thought that I was possibly in some kind of danger. I thought that they might come to visit me, and I thought that it would be best for me if I could tell them that I hadn't told the police all of the details. That's why I concealed all of this from you when we met before. That's why I made up some stories to tell you. I thought that Mr. Ishihara and the syndicates might come to see me."

"But the news of Mr. Ishihara's suicide this morning has scared me even more, and that's what made me decide to come and talk to you. I guess that the syndicates must know about me by now. Perhaps they know about the plan that I made with Atsushi? Perhaps they know that we'd been trying to run away with the money? I feel as though I'm in increasing danger from the syndicates myself."

Morimoto slowly shook his head.

"No, I don't think so, Ms. Sakai. I don't think so at all. I don't think that you've anything to worry about now. You've nothing to worry about at all. I don't think that you're in even the slightest bit of danger from the syndicates. The more that I find out about this whole incident, the more I feel that it has absolutely nothing to do with the syndicates at all."

CHAPTER 19

▼

Ms. Sakai had provided an enthralling account of the events surrounding Mr. Sekikawa's death for Inspector Morimoto and Police Officer Suzuki, and they were both anxious to learn some more of the details that they knew would be vital in determining who had actually committed the murder.

"Ms. Sakai," Morimoto said, "I'm very grateful that you decided to come and talk to us this morning. And as I said, I'm really quite sure that there's nothing further for you to worry about concerning your own safety. What you've told us will certainly help us in our investigation of Mr. Sekikawa's murder."

"I'm very glad of that," Ms. Sakai replied. "I'd like to see his killers brought to justice. But actually, I'm rather confused. You said that you thought the syndicates weren't involved at all. If the syndicates didn't kill Atsushi, then who did? And why did they kill him?"

"Well, that's what Officer Suzuki and I are doing our very best to find out, Ms. Sakai. And before you leave, it would be helpful if I could ask you a few questions. There are some details of the events at Okayama station that you witnessed that I'm particularly interested in, and which will be very useful for us as we try to determine who really did kill Mr. Sekikawa."

"Oh, please ask me anything, Inspector, anything at all. I want to give you as much help as I possibly can."

"Thank you, Ms. Sakai. Well then, to start off with, perhaps you could think back to when you were waiting at the bus stop outside the station. You said that you saw Mr. Sekikawa arrive at Momotaro's statue, didn't you?"

"Yes, that's right. I was there when he arrived, but as I said, I didn't speak to him."

"Yes. It was raining that evening, wasn't it? You said that Mr. Sekikawa was using an umbrella?"

"Yes, he was."

"Do you remember what kind of umbrella it was?"

"Oh yes, it was his own umbrella, a dark green one. I think that I told you about it before. He'd had it with him that morning when we'd taken the train from Kurashiki to Okayama."

"I see. And then after a while, somebody came out to the statue to meet Mr. Sekikawa, you said. I'm wondering, did they chat for a while at the statue? Did they stand and talk for a while? Do you remember?"

Ms. Sakai shook her head.

"No, as soon as they saw each other they left right away. I think that they must have been talking to each other as they walked to the hotel. It seemed to me as though it was the person that Atsushi had been expecting, so naturally I thought that it was Mr. Ishihara. Anyway, as soon as they saw each other, the person, whoever it was, immediately led Atsushi away towards the hotel."

"I suppose that the person who met Mr. Sekikawa must have had an umbrella with him as well, isn't that right?"

"Oh yes, he had one as well. I remember that it was raining quite hard."

"Do you recall what kind of umbrella it was?"

Ms. Sakai thought for a moment.

"I can remember, yes. It was quite similar to Atsushi's umbrella, but it was a different color. It was red, dark red."

"I see. You're quite sure about that, are you?"

"Yes, I'm quite sure."

Morimoto looked over at Suzuki.

"Officer Suzuki, I wonder whether you wouldn't mind…"

Suzuki interrupted Morimoto before he could finish his sentence.

"Yes, of course, sir. I'll go and get it right away."

Suzuki left the room and came back shortly with Mr. Ishihara's dark red umbrella which she placed upon the table in front of Ms. Sakai.

"Could this have been the umbrella that you saw?" Morimoto asked.

Ms. Sakai looked at the umbrella and shrugged.

"Yes, it could have been. That's certainly the right color. The man who met Atsushi had an umbrella just like this."

"Thank you."

Morimoto rubbed his chin and considered his next question.

"Now, Ms. Sakai, you said that you followed them both into the lobby of the Grandview Hotel, and you saw them enter an elevator."

"That's right. They took one of the elevators that goes up to the hotel rooms and restaurants."

"Did they still have their umbrellas with them when they walked into the elevator?"

Ms. Sakai frowned and thought.

"Well, they did, yes. When they entered the hotel, they closed their umbrellas, of course, and they carried them with them in the lobby and when they entered the elevator."

"They didn't leave the umbrellas in an umbrella stand at the hotel entrance, perhaps?"

"Oh, no. They didn't do that. I was watching them."

"What about when they came out of the elevator afterwards? They left the hotel and went to the coin locker, didn't they? Do you remember whether they had their umbrellas with them then?"

Ms. Sakai thought again.

"Well, let me see. Actually, they shared an umbrella. I remember now. When they left the hotel, they shared the dark red umbrella. Mr. Ishihara held it over both of them. And Atsushi was carrying the umbrella that they put in the coin locker."

"Was Mr. Sekikawa carrying anything else? Did he have anything else with him besides the umbrella which he left in the coin locker?"

"No. The only thing that he was carrying with him was the umbrella that he put in the coin locker."

"I see. Thank you, that's very helpful. And after they'd left the umbrella in the coin locker, you watched them both leaving the station, didn't you?"

"Yes, that's when Atsushi left the key in the tissue for me, as they walked out of the station. They left the station together, but I didn't follow them."

"Did they use an umbrella when they left the station?"

"Yes, they were still sharing the dark red umbrella."

Morimoto nodded and rubbed his chin again. There were a few moments of silence while Morimoto thought.

"Well, thank you, Ms. Sakai. Perhaps I could ask you one last question. The umbrella that you retrieved from the coin locker at Okayama station, and which you eventually threw into the Asahi River—what kind of umbrella was it?"

"Well, it was a big umbrella. It had the documents and the little plastic box wrapped inside it. It was rather like this umbrella here."

Ms. Sakai motioned towards Mr. Ishihara's umbrella that was lying in the middle of the table.

"But it was a different color," she added. "It was black."

Later that day, Morimoto was sitting in his office reviewing the new developments in the case. Lying on his desk in front of him was the envelope that he had received from Ms. Sakai. He had known what was inside it as soon as Ms. Sakai had mentioned that she had found it inside the umbrella that had been left in the coin locker at Okayama station. It contained copies of secret documents from National Electronics together with one of the computer chips that Mr. Ishihara had stolen, the computer chip that was still missing, the computer chip that was the center of Mr. Nishi's investigation, the computer chip that Mr. Nishi's Special Branch team had been so fervently searching for at Mr. Ishihara's office and home the previous evening.

Morimoto picked up the phone.

"Sergeant Yamada?"

"Yes, sir."

"Do you know whether the Chief is in now?"

"Err...yes, he is, sir."

"And Mr. Nishi, is he here as well?"

"Yes, sir, they're both upstairs in the Chief's office."

"Oh good, thank you."

Morimoto put down the phone and picked up the envelope from his desk. He walked out of his office and took the elevator to the seventh floor.

"I understand that the Chief is in, with Mr. Nishi," he said to the secretary sitting outside the Chief's office. "I just need a moment with them, please."

"Of course, Inspector Morimoto," the secretary replied, and knocked on the Chief's door.

"Yes, what is it?" the Chief replied.

"Inspector Morimoto would like to see you, sir," the secretary said.

Morimoto walked into the Chief's office. Mr. Nishi was in his usual seat next to the Chief, and like the Chief he looked even more exhausted and worn out than in the morning.

"Yes, what is it Morimoto?" the Chief asked in a tired voice. "What is it that you want to see me about? I thought that we'd been over everything this morning?"

"Well, actually, sir, it's really Mr. Nishi that I want to see."

Morimoto smiled at Mr. Nishi and held out the brown envelope.

"This is for you, Mr. Nishi."

Mr. Nishi stared back in bewilderment.

"It's copies of some secret documents from National Electronics. Oh, and I almost forgot…the missing computer chip is in the envelope as well. I thought that you might be looking for it."

CHAPTER 20

▼

The next time that Inspector Morimoto and Police Officer Suzuki were together in their office was the following Monday morning. The weekend had been particularly busy for both of them. First there had been Mr. Ishihara's suicide, and that had been followed by Ms. Sakai's remarkable account of her plan and the events that had occurred on the evening of Mr. Sekikawa's murder.

And perhaps most important of all, there was the recovery of the computer chip together with the documents from National Electronics that Ms. Sakai had delivered to Morimoto. These materials had finally established a link between Mr. Sekikawa's murder and Mr. Ishihara's industrial espionage, and they had been of especial interest to the Chief and Mr. Nishi.

At last Morimoto had been able to get some time to himself, and he had taken up his favorite position. His legs were resting up on his desk, his chair was inclined backwards, and his hands were locked behind his neck. Suzuki was sitting at her desk.

"Well, Suzuki, we now know the answers to several of our puzzles. The mystery of why Ms. Sakai closed her bank account, the mystery of the whereabouts of Mr. Sekikawa's umbrella, and most interesting of all, the mystery of why Mr. Sekikawa was carrying the key to an empty coin locker. We now have reasonable explanations for all of those questions."

Suzuki nodded.

"Yes, sir, that's right."

"It was rather an ingenious plan that Mr. Sekikawa and Ms. Sakai came up with, don't you think, Suzuki? I don't expect that too many people would have been able to think up an idea like that."

"Yes, sir, I agree. It was a rather clever plan. However, it obviously didn't succeed, and I wonder at what point it broke down. When Mr. Sekikawa was killed, do you think that his murderer or murderers were aware that the keys had been switched? Do you think that they even knew that Mr. Sekikawa had a key at all?"

"Yes, quite. There are several important points about the case that are still unclear."

Morimoto stared out of the window at the bright blue sky. After a few moments, he made another comment.

"You know, Suzuki, the rest of this case is going to be all about umbrellas. What we have to do now is count up all of the umbrellas."

Later that morning there was a loud thumping on the door and the Chief bounded into the office with a big grin on his face.

"Hello, Morimoto and Suzuki! I just wanted to stop by to say well done! That was fantastic work recovering those documents and the missing computer chip. And we certainly showed Special Branch a thing or two there, didn't we! I'm sure that won't go unnoticed in Tokyo. I don't think they'll be underestimating the Okayama Police Department in the future, I'll say!"

The Chief looked at Morimoto and Suzuki with evident joy.

"I suppose that Mr. Nishi would have found the missing chip in the end, though, one way or another. Special Branch was certainly putting in enough work. They were looking for it in Mr. Ishihara's office, and at his home as well. But you beat them to it, didn't you, Morimoto! Fantastic work! Mr. Nishi seemed quite taken aback, didn't he? He was at a complete loss for words…rendered utterly speechless. Anyway, he's back in Tokyo now. His investigation is over now that the second computer chip has been recovered."

"By the way, Morimoto, it's a very strange set of events that you told us. I mean the documents and the computer chip being hidden in an umbrella and all that. Who'd have believed it? And after all, it seems that this leaking from National Electronics was connected to Mr. Sekikawa's murder. I do hope that you can get to the bottom of that as well."

The Chief bounded out of the room and Morimoto smiled at Suzuki.

"Well, Suzuki, the Chief's in a good mood today, isn't he? Perhaps it's because Special Branch have finally packed up and gone back to Tokyo?"

Suzuki laughed.

Morimoto looked at his watch.

"You know, Suzuki, it's about lunch time, isn't it? I was thinking that we might go out for a spot of lunch somewhere. I'm sure the Chief feels that we deserve it. I was rather thinking of the Grandview Hotel, as a matter of fact. How about it, Suzuki?"

"Sounds like a wonderful idea, sir."

The rainy season in Okayama was coming to an end, and it was bright and sunny, with an occasional fluffy white cumulus cloud floating in the sky. The tram ride from police headquarters to Okayama station did not take Morimoto and Suzuki very long, and when they stepped off the tram they walked over to the statue of Momotaro.

"She'd have had a reasonable view from over there, wouldn't she," Morimoto said, pointing over to the bus stops.

"Ms. Sakai, sir? Yes, she'd have been able to see what happened quite clearly, I think."

The Grandview Hotel is located at the southern end of the Okayama station building, and as they walked from Momotaro's statue towards the hotel entrance, Morimoto and Suzuki retraced the steps that Mr. Sekikawa and his visitor from Osaka had taken on the evening of Mr. Sekikawa's murder. It only took them a minute to reach the hotel.

The Grandview Hotel is one of the premier hotels in Okayama. It soars high above Okayama station with two large buildings that are joined together at an obtuse angle of about one hundred and twenty-five degrees. The hotel facade is smooth and white, with small square windows. Underneath the hotel, there are three floors of parking garages, and the wide spacious lobby is on the first floor, together with various shops and cafes. There are then four additional floors of restaurants, shops and banquet halls that are used for wedding parties and other such events. Above these are eleven floors of guest rooms, and then the top floor of the hotel contains several additional restaurants.

Morimoto and Suzuki walked through the two automatic curved glass doors at the hotel entrance. In the middle of the spacious lobby was an assortment of sofas and comfortable chairs, and there was a long reception desk over on the right hand side. A souvenir shop in the corner of the lobby was displaying grapes and peaches, together with some fine pieces of the locally produced Bizen pottery, with its distinctive coarse, rustic appearance.

Just as Mr. Sekikawa and his visitor had done two and a half weeks previously, Morimoto and Suzuki turned right and walked across the white marble floor to a small vestibule at the side of the lobby that contained four elevators. They rode one of the elevators up to the top floor where they were able to obtain a window table at one of the restaurants. From their seats, they could look directly down onto the top of Okayama station, and in particular they had an unobstructed view along the bullet train tracks and platforms.

Morimoto and Suzuki both ordered a tempura set lunch. These arrived on large trays, and consisted of an assortment of dishes of various sizes. There was a bowl of rice, a small dish of pickles, a bowl of hot fermented soybean soup containing tofu and seaweed, and there was a cup of hot green tea. And then there was the tempura, which was large pieces of shrimp, pumpkin, eggplant, green pepper and onions, which had been coated with batter and deep-fried. Next to the tempura was a dark colored dipping sauce, made from soy sauce, rice wine and other flavorings. There was also a pile of grated radish that Morimoto and Suzuki added to their dipping sauce before beginning their meal.

While they were enjoying their lunch, Morimoto and Suzuki watched the bullet trains arriving and departing from the station below them. The trains that arrived at the station from beneath the hotel, and which left the station heading away from where they were sitting, were the trains that had come from Hiroshima and which were heading towards Osaka. These trains traveled on the left of the two adjacent bullet train tracks.

The trains traveling in the opposite direction were on the right hand track. These were the trains that they could see arriving in the distance through Okayama city, decelerating as they pulled into the station. As they departed they disappeared beneath the hotel. These trains were heading towards Hiroshima.

After they had finished their meal, Morimoto spoke to Suzuki about the case.

"I think that it has to have been Mr. Ishihara who met Mr. Sekikawa at the station that evening, don't you, Suzuki?"

Suzuki nodded as she stirred her coffee.

"Yes, sir, I think that it was Mr. Ishihara. We can't be sure, of course, but it makes the most sense. And the phone call on Wednesday night must have been from Mr. Ishihara as well. Mr. Sekikawa would have been able to recognize his voice, and we know that Mr. Ishihara had the opportunity to make the call from Osaka station. Since Mr. Ishihara said that he was coming to Okayama, that's who Mr. Sekikawa was expecting. And from what Ms. Sakai told us, it seems that Mr. Sekikawa was met by the person who he was expecting."

"And on top of all that," Suzuki continued, "there's the umbrella, Mr. Ishihara's dark red umbrella. Ms. Sakai clearly identified the person as having an umbrella just like Mr. Ishihara's."

"Yes, that's right," Morimoto agreed.

Suzuki sipped her coffee.

"However," she added, "from what Ms. Sakai told us, it seems as though Mr. Ishihara must have been wearing some form of disguise. But that's probably not very surprising. After all, if it really was him then he'd apparently gone to great lengths to devise this plan. If Mr. Ishihara had come up with this clandestine scheme so that he could visit Okayama for just one hour, while being able to give the impression that he was at the baseball game in the Osaka Dome, then he wouldn't have wanted to take the chance that somebody might recognize him. He wouldn't have wanted to have been recognized on the train, or in Okayama, or at the station in Osaka."

"Yes, I agree."

"In any case, sir, it's not that difficult to come up with a simple form of disguise. From what Ms. Sakai told us, it sounds as though Mr. Ishihara just used a hairpiece, a false mustache and some glasses. I suppose that he'd have put on his disguise before leaving the Osaka Dome. He probably did it in the public bathroom. And he'd have removed his disguise when he was back in Osaka, before returning to his hotel."

"That sounds quite plausible."

"And furthermore," Suzuki continued, "Mr. Sekikawa was expecting Mr. Ishihara to meet him at the station. So I suppose that Mr. Sekikawa would have been able to tell easily enough that the person who met him was really just Mr. Ishihara wearing a disguise. At least, when they were close together he'd have seen that it was Mr. Ishihara. They knew each other very well, after all, and Mr. Sekikawa did follow the person here to the hotel."

"Yes, Suzuki, that's a key point, isn't it? Why did they come here? According to Ms. Sakai, they were here for only five minutes or so. That wasn't very long. But whatever they did here had something to do with exchanging umbrellas. Mr. Sekikawa arrived with his dark green umbrella but he left with a black umbrella. The trip to the hotel must have been an important part of Mr. Ishihara's plan, don't you think?"

"Yes, sir, it must have been. Ms. Sakai was very clear about the umbrellas. When Mr. Sekikawa and Mr. Ishihara, if that's who it really was, came here they had two umbrellas with them, the dark red one and the dark green one. But then, according to Ms. Sakai, when they left here Mr. Sekikawa was carrying the black umbrella and the other person still had their dark red umbrella. But they only had those two umbrellas. The black umbrella, of course, had the documents and the computer chip inside it, and they deposited it in the coin locker in the station. Eventually, Ms. Sakai threw it into the river a few days afterwards."

Morimoto nodded.

"Anyway," Suzuki continued, "it looks as though Mr. Ishihara brought Mr. Sekikawa here in order to collect the black umbrella. In the process, it also seems as though Mr. Sekikawa left his dark green umbrella here. After they'd deposited the black umbrella in the coin locker, they only had one umbrella left between the two of them."

Morimoto and Suzuki drank their coffee.

"The matter which we have to consider now," Morimoto said, "is whereabouts in the hotel did they go? I think that Mr. Ishihara must have had a room here, don't you?"

"Yes, sir, a room seems quite likely. On the other hand, it's also possible that they met somebody in one of the restaurants, somebody who'd brought the black umbrella with them. But if nobody else was involved, then it seems that Mr. Ishihara must have stored the black umbrella here in the hotel, and therefore it would appear as though he must have had a room here. Mr. Ishihara must have had a room here where he'd left the umbrella."

"It's unfortunate," Suzuki continued, "that we don't know which floor they went to in the elevator. In the lobby, there's no way to determine which floor the elevators are on, so even if Ms. Sakai had tried to find out which floor they went to, she wouldn't have been able to tell. However, sir, we do know that they didn't go to one of the parking garages in the basement. That's because access to the basement garages is from a different set of elevators, over on the other side of the lobby. So we do at least know that Mr. Sekikawa and Mr. Ishihara came up from the lobby to one of the higher floors."

"Yes, it would be nice to know which floor they came to," Morimoto agreed. "But anyhow, let's suppose that Mr. Ishihara did have a room here. Given the lengths to which he'd gone to keep his trip here a secret, I think that we can quite safely assume that he'd have obtained the room under a different name, don't you think so?"

"Definitely, sir. It seems clear that Mr. Ishihara wouldn't have checked into the hotel using his own name. He'd have used a false name."

"Nevertheless, Suzuki, I think that we can deduce something about the dates that he'd have been able to check in and check out of the hotel, can't we?"

"Yes, that's right, sir. Mr. Ishihara would have needed to reserve his room here before he left on his business trip to Osaka. He wouldn't have had time to check in on Thursday night before he met Mr. Sekikawa. He left early on Wednesday morning, so that means that he'd have had to have checked in here on Tuesday, say, or maybe even before that."

Morimoto nodded.

"And when would he have checked out?"

"Well, sir, Friday night is possible, I suppose, but unlikely I think. When Mr. Ishihara returned to Okayama on the bullet train from Osaka that Friday afternoon, our police car met him and took him directly to headquarters where you talked with him. After that, he returned to National Electronics in another police car that you arranged for him."

"After he returned to his office," Suzuki continued, "I'd have thought that Mr. Ishihara would have been very busy. He'd have had to deal with all of the arrangements relating to the death of Mr. Sekikawa, all of the arrangements that needed to be handled by the company. I think, therefore, that it's much more likely that Mr. Ishihara would have checked out of the hotel room on Saturday morning."

"Yes, I think that you're right," Morimoto agreed.

They had finished their coffee and they stood up and walked over to the cashier to pay their bill. While they were waiting by the elevators to ride back down to the lobby, Morimoto turned to Suzuki.

"You know, I think that we might pay a visit to the hotel manager. How about it, Suzuki?"

CHAPTER 21

▼

"It was room sixteen hundred and three, sir," Police Officer Suzuki announced to Inspector Morimoto as she walked into their office. "Room sixteen hundred and three at the Grandview Hotel."

It was late in the afternoon on Tuesday, the day after Morimoto and Suzuki had taken lunch together at the Grandview Hotel. They had been able to meet the hotel manager after their lunch, and he had been quite happy to help them. Morimoto and Suzuki had explained that they were trying to trace somebody who they believed might have had a room at the hotel on the Thursday night two weeks before. The manager had told them that the hotel would do whatever it could to cooperate with their investigation, and he had provided Suzuki with the hotel registration cards for all of the guests who had stayed on the Thursday evening.

Suzuki sat down at her desk with a satisfied smile on her face.

"Not only does it seem that it was room sixteen hundred and three, sir, but there are also some suggestions that it really was Mr. Ishihara who was using the room."

Morimoto was pleased. He got up from his desk and went over to the teapot on the table in the middle of the office. He poured a cup of tea and took it over to Suzuki's desk for her.

"That's very interesting," Morimoto said, smiling. "Please tell me how you've been able to discover the room number. Please tell me all of the details."

Morimoto sat down again, loosened his tie, and rested his legs up on the corner of his desk.

"Well, sir, first of all it was the only phony address among all of the hotel registration cards. The Grandview Hotel has a total of three hundred and twenty-eight rooms, but only slightly more than half of them were occupied on that Thursday night. So, actually, I had a little less than two hundred registration cards to examine."

"Luckily," Suzuki continued, "I was able to obtain some help from the hotel staff, and together we checked all of the addresses and phone numbers on the registration cards. The hotel staff knew quite a lot of the people, and I called some of the other people myself, just to check that there wasn't anything suspicious about them. Everybody seemed quite genuine. Everybody, that is, except for one person."

"There wasn't anything suspicious about any of the hotel guests that evening, except for this one room. It was a single room on the sixteenth floor that had been taken by a man called Mr. Kuroki. He'd written down his occupation as businessman. The thing is, though, he'd given a false address and a false telephone number in Tokyo. The address doesn't even exist and the telephone number isn't in use. I checked into them myself."

Morimoto nodded.

"That sounds like the kind of person that we're looking for, Suzuki. What about the handwriting? Have you had the handwriting on the registration card examined?"

"Yes, sir. The handwriting has been examined, although the results aren't very conclusive, I'm afraid. I showed the handwriting on Mr. Kuroki's hotel registration card to our experts here, and they compared it with some of Mr. Ishihara's handwriting. However, they said that they really couldn't say anything, one way or the other. Mr. Ishihara wrote with his right hand, but Mr. Kuroki had filled out the hotel registration card using his left hand."

"Hmmm...I see," Morimoto said. "And what about the check in time? The registration card would have recorded Mr. Kuroki's check in time, wouldn't it? And what about the check out time? Do they tie in with what we know about Mr. Ishihara?"

"Yes, sir, in fact they're pretty much what we'd predicted they'd be when we discussed the possibility yesterday over lunch. It seems that Mr. Kuroki checked into the Grandview Hotel at seven thirty on Tuesday evening. That was the evening just before Mr. Ishihara left on his business trip to Osaka. Mr. Kuroki paid for the room in advance with cash when he checked in."

"I telephoned National Electronics, sir, and I spoke with Mr. Ishihara's secretary. She said that her records show that Mr. Ishihara left his office that evening just after seven o'clock. That would have given him plenty of time to reach the Grandview Hotel by seven thirty. The hotel is on his way home, actually."

"Was anybody at the hotel able to give you a physical description of Mr. Kuroki?" Morimoto asked. "Did you talk to any of the receptionists who were working at that time?"

"Unfortunately, sir, it turns out that nobody can remember him in any detail. I did try to get a physical description of him, though. I talked to the receptionists who'd been working when Mr. Kuroki checked in and out of the hotel, but nobody could remember much about him."

"I'm not really surprised," Morimoto said. "If it really was Mr. Ishihara, then he certainly wouldn't have been trying to draw attention to himself."

"Not at all, sir. And in addition, I suppose that if it really were Mr. Ishihara, then presumably he'd have been wearing his disguise. He wouldn't have wanted to be recognized, not if he was using a false name and address, so he'd probably have been wearing the same disguise that he appears to have been wearing on the Thursday evening when he met Mr. Sekikawa."

"Yes, I expect so. When did Mr. Kuroki check out of the hotel then?"

"Again, sir, just as we predicted. He checked out on Saturday morning, at 9:20. And that does tie in with Mr. Ishihara's itinerary as well. His secretary told me that her records show that he arrived at his office just before ten o'clock on that Saturday morning."

"I suppose, sir, that after leaving home on that Saturday morning, Mr. Ishihara would have gone straight to the Grandview Hotel to check out of his room—Mr. Kuroki's room, that is. And first he'd have needed to find somewhere to put on his disguise. Then after checking out of the hotel, he could have removed his disguise at Okayama station, perhaps. After that, he could have gone straight to his office. The times all fit in with each other."

Morimoto was nodding.

"So do you think that Mr. Ishihara and Mr. Kuroki are in fact one and the same person, then?" he asked. "And do you think that Mr. Ishihara took Mr. Sekikawa up to room sixteen hundred and three? Do you think that's where they went after meeting each other at the station?"

Suzuki shrugged.

"As far as I can see, sir, there's nothing to suggest that it couldn't have happened like that. And actually, sir, there's an additional point that's quite interesting, I think. The maid who cleaned the room during that period has the records of the linen changes that she made. I had a look at them this morning."

"It turns out, sir, that the maid changed the bed sheets and towels in that room on every day except for Thursday. Her records showed that when she cleaned the room on Thursday she hadn't changed the sheets and towels. She hadn't changed them because they hadn't needed to be changed. In other words, the room hadn't been used on the Wednesday evening. Or to be more specific, sir, the room hadn't been used at all between the time when she'd cleaned it on Wednesday and the time when she went to clean the room again on Thursday."

"Ah, that is rather interesting," Morimoto said, smiling. "Very interesting indeed. Moreover, it's also interesting that she'd needed to change the sheets on the other days, isn't it? According to our theory, if Mr. Kuroki really was Mr. Ishihara, then the room would never have actually been slept in at all, would it?"

"That's correct, sir. But if our theory is correct, then we have a pretty good idea of the precise times when Mr. Ishihara was in that room. It seems to me that he'd have been in the room exactly three times. The first time would have been when he checked into the hotel on Tuesday evening, the second time would have been when Mr. Ishihara went to the room on Thursday evening with Mr. Sekikawa, and the third and final time would have been when he checked out of the hotel on Saturday morning. At each of those three times, Mr. Ishihara's visit to the room was probably only very brief. Nevertheless, he'd have been able to mess up the room a bit if he'd wanted to."

Morimoto nodded.

"It would only have been necessary," Suzuki continued, "for Mr. Ishihara to pull the bed sheets around a bit, and to get the towels wet—just something to give the impression that the room was being used. And that's why the maid changed the linen just three times. The first time was Wednesday, the second time was Friday, and the third time was after Mr. Kuroki, or whoever it was, had checked out of the room on Saturday morning."

"However," Suzuki added, "according to our theory of what might have happened, Mr. Ishihara wouldn't have been able to go to the room between the time when the maid went to clean it on Wednesday morning, and when she went to clean it again on Thursday morning. Mr. Ishihara would have been in Osaka all of that time. And that coincides precisely with the maid's records that she didn't need to change the linen on Thursday."

Suzuki sat back in her chair feeling quite contented. She was pleased that she had been able to find a room at the Grandview Hotel which seemed to be consistent with their idea that Mr. Ishihara had taken a room there, and she especially liked the way that the linen changes fitted in with their theory that Mr. Kuroki might have been Mr. Ishihara.

"Well, if our theory is correct," Morimoto said, "then the black umbrella must have already been in the room on Thursday night when Mr. Sekikawa and Mr. Ishihara went up there. And when they left the room, they must have left Mr. Sekikawa's dark green umbrella behind."

"Yes, that's right, sir. That would mean that Mr. Ishihara must have taken the black umbrella with him when he checked into the hotel on Tuesday evening, and he must have left it in the room at that time."

"Incidentally, Suzuki, was there anything left behind in the room when Mr. Kuroki checked out on Saturday morning?"

"No, sir, there wasn't. That's something that I checked with the hotel as well. They say that they keep records of anything left behind in the rooms, and apparently Mr. Kuroki didn't leave anything behind in his room."

Morimoto and Suzuki sat in silence for a while, thinking about the implications of what they had been discussing. Eventually, Morimoto looked across at Suzuki again and spoke up.

"Well, Suzuki, we're going to have to address the question of whether it's possible that it was Mr. Ishihara who killed Mr. Sekikawa. And if he did kill him, did he do it by himself, and what was his motive? And furthermore, we have to consider what part, if any, the syndicates really played in all of this."

"Well, sir, I think that I feel the same way as you do about the role that the syndicates played in this murder case. Last Saturday you told Ms. Sakai that you thought that the syndicates probably weren't involved at all, and I really believe that you could be right. However, we do know that the syndicates received money for the first computer chip that was recovered by Special Branch. And since Mr. Ishihara was responsible for stealing the chips from his company, that does seem to indicate a link between Mr. Ishihara and the syndicates. Nevertheless, we have to ask ourselves whether there really are any direct links between Mr. Sekikawa's murder and the syndicates."

"You see, sir, if we think back to the very beginning of the case, the syndicates first entered the story because of the way in which Mr. Sekikawa was killed—he'd had his throat cut in the traditional syndicate style, and the knife had been placed on his chest pointing towards his throat. And after that we discovered that Mr. Sekikawa was in trouble with the syndicates. We discovered that he owed them a lot of money. That was why it initially seemed to everybody that the syndicates were responsible for the murder."

"And then, sir, the next time that the syndicates were linked to the case was when Ms. Sakai told us that Mr. Sekikawa had arranged to meet them on Thursday night. However, it turns out that, as we suspected, she'd made up that part of her story. It was a complete fabrication. The telephone call to Mr. Sekikawa's apartment on Wednesday night had come from Mr. Ishihara, not from the syndicates. Therefore, the only other real link between the murder and the syndicates is that, according to Ms. Sakai, Mr. Ishihara told Mr. Sekikawa that he'd arranged a meeting with the syndicates on Thursday evening."

"Precisely," Morimoto said. "That's precisely right."

"However," Suzuki continued, "that was quite possibly an invention of Mr. Ishihara. It's quite possible that Mr. Ishihara hadn't contacted the syndicates at all. And, if there wasn't a meeting arranged with the syndicates on Thursday night, then there's actually no link to the syndicates at all. There's only the appearance that the syndicates are involved because it was a syndicate style killing of somebody who was in deep trouble with the syndicates."

"Yes, I agree with you, Suzuki. In other words, the real killer may have had nothing to do with the syndicates, but they just wanted to leave the impression that it was a syndicate murder. After all, the way in which the syndicates carry out an assassination is hardly a secret. It's practically common knowledge, really. So the killer could easily have found out how to copy it."

Suzuki nodded.

"Yes, that's right, sir. And obviously, the motive for copying the syndicates' method of assassination could have been that the killer wanted to give the impression that it was a syndicate murder in order to shift attention away from themselves."

CHAPTER 22

▼

Inspector Morimoto removed his glasses and rubbed his eyes. It was by now quite late on Tuesday afternoon, and the sun would soon be disappearing behind the Okayama skyline. Morimoto replaced his glasses and scratched his head.

He reflected on the plan that Ms. Sakai had made with Mr. Sekikawa. It fitted in well with the facts of the case that they knew. What remained was to piece together a plan for Mr. Ishihara that would also fit in with everything that they knew. The final resolution of the murder case seemed to depend upon clarifying what Mr. Ishihara had been doing, and Police Officer Suzuki's discovery of Mr. Kuroki's room at the Grandview Hotel appeared to be an important part of the puzzle.

"Well, Suzuki, there doesn't seem to be any other alternative than to consider that whoever met Mr. Sekikawa next to Momotaro's statue that evening must be our prime suspect. He must be the most likely candidate to have committed the murder. That person, whoever it may have been, was the last person seen with Mr. Sekikawa while he was still alive. Ms. Sakai said that she watched them walk away from the station together."

Suzuki nodded.

"Yes, sir, we've no evidence that Mr. Sekikawa met anybody else that night. So it seems almost certain that the person who he left the station with must have been involved in the murder one way or another, and they may very well have actually committed the murder."

"And moreover, Suzuki, the chances are that it was Mr. Ishihara who met Mr. Sekikawa, and so that implies that Mr. Ishihara is the prime suspect for having killed Mr. Sekikawa. The question is, why did he do it?"

"Well, sir, it's not difficult to imagine why Mr. Ishihara might have had a motive for killing Mr. Sekikawa. An obvious possibility is that Mr. Sekikawa had found out that Mr. Ishihara was leaking the company secrets. Perhaps Mr. Sekikawa confronted him? Perhaps he even tried to blackmail him? That would provide Mr. Ishihara with a clear motive for getting rid of Mr. Sekikawa."

"And in that case," Suzuki continued, "if Mr. Ishihara was being blackmailed, that could explain why he'd decided to raise some money in Osaka for Mr. Sekikawa. It wasn't for friendship's sake, to help out a friend in his division. Instead it was so that Mr. Sekikawa wouldn't spill the beans. It was so that Mr. Sekikawa wouldn't turn him in. The problem is, though, that doesn't fit in with Ms. Sakai and Mr. Sekikawa's plan. If Mr. Ishihara was actually bringing money for Mr. Sekikawa, to pay him off so that he'd keep quiet, there'd be no need for all of that business with the switching of the coin locker keys."

Morimoto thought back to his meeting with the Chief, and he remembered that the Chief had described Mr. Ishihara as a thief and a traitor. Morimoto wondered whether Mr. Ishihara was actually a murderer, as well. Would Mr. Ishihara really have gone so far as to kill somebody? Would he have killed somebody who worked under him at National Electronics? Could he have stood behind Mr. Sekikawa and drawn the kitchen knife through his throat?

"If Mr. Kuroki and Mr. Ishihara were in fact the same person," Morimoto said, "then where does that leave us? It means that Mr. Ishihara devised and carried out a rather intricate plan of his own. We know that he'd stolen two of National Electronics' secret computer chips and that he'd been making copies of sensitive documents, and we know that he'd been able to make a lot of money from selling them. That's what Mr. Nishi's investigation found out."

"Yes, sir."

"And furthermore, we also know that Mr. Ishihara realized that somebody had found out about the leaks, and that he knew that an investigation was being carried out. In fact, according to the Chief, Mr. Ishihara most probably knew that an investigation of his whole division at National Electronics was being conducted by Special Branch."

"That's right, sir. And specifically, the Chief told you that Mr. Ishihara would have known for some time that he himself was under suspicion for the leaks."

"Exactly," Morimoto replied. "So I believe that Mr. Ishihara made a plan of his own, a plan that ultimately led to murder. Let's see if we can reconstruct Mr. Ishihara's plan ourselves. I think that it must have started one day when Mr. Ishihara contacted Mr. Sekikawa and told him that he'd found a way to help him pay back some of his debts, just as Ms. Sakai said that he'd done. I think that it began when Mr. Ishihara told Mr. Sekikawa that he was going to help him pay back some of the money that he owed the syndicates."

Suzuki nodded.

"And so," Morimoto continued, "Mr. Ishihara told Mr. Sekikawa that he'd probably be able to collect the money from one of his business contacts during his next trip to Osaka. And he told Mr. Sekikawa to wait for a telephone call from him on Wednesday night. But, Mr. Ishihara cautioned Mr. Sekikawa not to tell anybody else about what they were doing. When Mr. Sekikawa agreed, Mr. Ishihara was ready to put his plan into action."

"The first stage of Mr. Ishihara's plan went into effect after he left his office on Tuesday afternoon. He donned a disguise and he checked into the Grandview Hotel under a false name, Mr. Kuroki, being careful to invent a false address and telephone number in Tokyo for the hotel registration card, which he filled out with his left hand even though he was naturally right-handed. After checking in, he went up to his room and he messed up the linen somewhat. And he also left a black umbrella in the room. Inside the umbrella he'd wrapped the computer chip together with copies of some documents relating to its production. Then Mr. Ishihara left the hotel, found somewhere to remove his disguise, and went home just as usual on that Tuesday evening."

"On Wednesday morning, Mr. Ishihara took the Nozomi bullet train to Osaka for his business trip, and in his luggage he carried his disguise, a radio with headphones, and the sharp kitchen knife. Nothing unusual happened on Wednesday, except that after Mr. Ishihara had finished his dinner with his hosts from Consolidated Chipboards, he stopped off at Osaka station on the way back to his hotel where he used a public telephone to make a telephone call to Mr. Sekikawa."

"Mr. Ishihara telephoned Mr. Sekikawa, who was waiting for the call in his apartment at Kurashiki, and he asked Mr. Sekikawa to meet him at seven thirty the next evening. And they arranged that Mr. Sekikawa should be waiting for him at Momotaro's statue outside Okayama station. Mr. Ishihara told Mr. Sekikawa that he'd bring the money with him. It was quite a lot of money, and Mr. Ishihara explained that after they'd put the money inside a coin locker, they'd go to meet the syndicates."

"Mr. Ishihara implied that he'd made the arrangements with the syndicates himself. He also asked Mr. Sekikawa to bring the key to a coin locker, a large coin locker at Okayama station. Mr. Ishihara knew that the large coin lockers are sufficiently big enough to accommodate an umbrella, an umbrella that won't fold up. Presumably, he didn't want to take the chance that they wouldn't be able to find one of the large lockers available."

Suzuki nodded.

"So then the next day," Morimoto continued, "which was Thursday, Mr. Ishihara made sure that he finished his work quite early. He needed to finish early enough for him to get back to the Crystal House Hotel before five thirty. Mr. Ishihara then made a point of chatting to the receptionists. He talked to them about how pleased he was that he could go to the baseball game that evening, and he asked them to order a taxi to take him to the Osaka Dome. His objective was to ensure that the receptionists would remember that he'd been going to watch the baseball game that evening."

"After a short visit to his hotel room, he came back down to the hotel lobby where his taxi was waiting for him, and concealed inside his jacket was his disguise and the kitchen knife. He also carried his dark red umbrella, and he had the radio in his pocket. He took the taxi to the Osaka Dome, and he knew that there'd be a game that evening, even though it was raining heavily. He bought a ticket for the game and he entered the dome together with the rest of the crowd, and Mr. Ishihara was careful to keep his ticket stub."

"But then Mr. Ishihara put on his disguise in the public bathroom and he walked out of the dome. He traveled to the Shin-Osaka station by subway train and he took the Nozomi bullet train back to Okayama. He reached Okayama just after seven thirty, and he went to meet Mr. Sekikawa at Momotaro's statue, just as they'd arranged. Up close, Mr. Sekikawa was surely able to recognize that it was Mr. Ishihara in disguise."

"Then, Mr. Ishihara led Mr. Sekikawa over to the Grandview Hotel where they went to the elevators and rode up to room sixteen hundred and three. When they were in the room, Mr. Ishihara messed up the bed sheets and the towels again, and then they left with the black umbrella, the black umbrella which had the computer chip and the copies of the documents concealed inside."

"Next, Mr. Ishihara and Mr. Sekikawa took the elevator back down to the hotel lobby and they walked out of the hotel. They went straight back towards the station, and inside the station they went to locker two hundred and three. Mr. Sekikawa took the key from his right pocket and opened up the locker, and they put the black umbrella inside. Then they paid three hundred yen into the locker, locked it up again and removed the key. Mr. Ishihara made sure that Mr. Sekikawa kept the key, which actually is what Mr. Sekikawa wanted to do anyway. Then they left the station, and Mr. Ishihara didn't notice that Mr. Sekikawa hid the key inside the tissue that he discarded in the trash can. Mr. Ishihara wouldn't have been expecting anything like that."

"So then we get to the part where the murder took place. Presumably, Mr. Ishihara led Mr. Sekikawa straight to the alley and killed him there. It was dark, and Mr. Ishihara just needed to get Mr. Sekikawa to a secluded place where he could attack him, and he didn't have much time to spare. Perhaps Mr. Ishihara managed to get him into the alley under the pretense that they were on their way to a meeting that had been arranged with the syndicates. We know now that Mr. Sekikawa had just been waiting for the right moment to run away and to make his escape, and we know that he'd been stalling for time so that Ms. Sakai could empty the coin locker. Mr. Sekikawa may have been worried about the syndicates, but he certainly wouldn't have been expecting Mr. Ishihara to attack him."

"Consequently, it's reasonable to believe that Mr. Sekikawa wouldn't have been on guard against Mr. Ishihara. Therefore, Mr. Sekikawa was taken by surprise, and that was his downfall. Mr. Ishihara took out his knife in his right hand and approached Mr. Sekikawa from behind...and slashed his throat. Mr. Sekikawa wouldn't have stood a chance. Mr. Ishihara was careful to do the killing exactly according to the syndicate style of assassination. He made sure that Mr. Sekikawa was left lying on his back with the knife on his chest, pointing up towards his mutilated throat."

"Of course, Mr. Ishihara would have wiped the knife clean of any fingerprints, and he'd also have needed to be careful not to get his clothes splashed with any blood. Ironically, before he was murdered Mr. Sekikawa believed that he himself had just tricked Mr. Ishihara by switching the coin locker keys. Mr. Sekikawa had been waiting for the right moment to make his escape to Takashima to meet Ms. Sakai, but unfortunately, he waited just a little too long."

"Anyway, we can suppose that after killing Mr. Sekikawa, Mr. Ishihara returned by himself to Okayama station as quickly as possible. He wanted to make sure that he was in time for the Nozomi bullet train that left Okayama at 8:32. I expect that Mr. Ishihara was in time for the train, and he rode it all the way back to Osaka. During the train ride he listened to his radio. It was probably just a very small radio with headphones that he kept in his pocket, but it enabled him to find out the status of the baseball game."

"When Mr. Ishihara arrived back in Osaka, he continued to keep track of the baseball game on his radio. The game would still have been going on, and he had to wait for about an hour and a half while the game went into extra innings. He may well have decided to take the subway back to the Osaka Dome. In any case, once the game had finished Mr. Ishihara calculated what would be the appropriate time to return to his hotel. On arrival at the hotel he wanted to give the impression that he'd just come from the Osaka Dome by taxi. And, of course, he removed his disguise before returning to the hotel."

"When Mr. Ishihara returned to the Crystal House Hotel, he again made a point of chatting with the receptionists. He showed them his ticket stub from the game and he boasted about the grand slam home run that he told them he'd seen. Actually, at the time that the grand slam home run was hit, Mr. Ishihara wasn't sitting in the Osaka Dome watching it. Instead he was in Okayama slitting Mr. Sekikawa's throat."

"The next day, Friday, Mr. Ishihara checked out of the Crystal House Hotel and went to visit Consolidated Chipboards in Osaka as usual. Towards the end of the morning, he received the telephone call from National Electronics that informed him of Mr. Sekikawa's death, and which indicated that the murder had apparently been carried out by the syndicates. Mr. Ishihara returned to Okayama as soon as possible, and he was driven here to the police station to talk with me."

Morimoto paused.

"And that's about it, Suzuki," he concluded, "except that on Saturday morning after leaving home, Mr. Ishihara went to Okayama station to put on his disguise again, and then he went to the Grandview Hotel. He went up to room sixteen hundred and three and messed up the sheets and the towels, and then he went and checked out of the hotel. He checked out under the name of Mr. Kuroki, of course. Afterwards, he removed his disguise and went to his office at National Electronics."

Morimoto looked over at Suzuki who had been listening intently.

"Yes, sir," Suzuki said and nodded. "That would appear to be about it. I suppose that would be how Mr. Ishihara's plan would have worked."

"It leaves us, though," Morimoto added, "with two rather important points to consider, doesn't it? Firstly, there's the question of Mr. Ishihara's motive. Why did he go to such lengths to carry out such a plan? Why did he go so far as to murder his colleague? And, secondly, there's the matter of whether there's any evidence for the events that I've described. What real evidence do we have that this is what actually happened?"

Suzuki nodded.

"Well, sir, with regard to the first point, I would think that Mr. Ishihara's motive is fairly clear. He presumably wanted to shift suspicion away from himself. Suspicion about the company leaks, that is. He was trying to frame Mr. Sekikawa. I believe it's as simple as that."

"Yes, exactly," Morimoto said. "I agree with you. I think that's correct."

"Assuming that Mr. Ishihara really did kill Mr. Sekikawa," Suzuki explained, "then at the moment when the murder took place, Mr. Ishihara wouldn't have known about the key switch. He wouldn't have known that Mr. Sekikawa was tricking him. Mr. Ishihara would have thought that when we found Mr. Sekikawa's body we'd find that he was carrying the key to the coin locker at Okayama station. Mr. Ishihara would have thought that we'd open the coin locker and that we'd discover the black umbrella with the missing computer chip and copies of the company documents inside it."

"Therefore, sir, it would be quite natural for us to conclude that it was Mr. Sekikawa who was responsible for the leaks from National Electronics. In fact, we'd probably have thought that Mr. Sekikawa was selling the chips and the documents in order to raise money to pay back his debts to the syndicates. It would have been such a natural explanation. What could be more obvious? We'd have reasoned that something must have gone wrong during Mr. Sekikawa's negotiations with the syndicates, something that had led to the syndicates killing him."

"And I suppose, sir, that Mr. Ishihara would have thought that once Mr. Sekikawa had been found with the missing chip and the documents, then the investigation into the leaking would stop. Mr. Ishihara would have hoped that he'd be safe from that point onwards. It's a very straightforward motive. Mr. Ishihara knew that Mr. Nishi's investigation had begun, and he was trying to make Mr. Sekikawa appear to be the culprit. That's why he came up with this elaborate plan."

"Absolutely," Morimoto agreed, "absolutely."

Morimoto thought back to his meeting with Mr. Ishihara at police headquarters on the day after the murder. If their theory was correct, then he had been sitting face to face with Mr. Sekikawa's murderer, less than twenty-four hours after the crime had been committed. He had been sitting with somebody who had just killed his own colleague in the hope that it would save his own skin, in the hope that it would save himself from being caught for selling national secrets abroad. And if their theory was correct, it meant that not only did Mr. Ishihara kill his colleague, but that he was also going to let his colleague be considered the traitor instead of himself.

"I suppose that if our conjecture really is correct," Morimoto said, "then Mr. Ishihara must have been rather confused in the days after the murder. He wouldn't have been able to understand why the investigations into the leaks were still continuing. He'd have thought that we'd found the computer chip and the documents concealed inside the umbrella in the coin locker at Okayama station."

"Yes, that's right, sir."

"Mr. Ishihara wouldn't have been able to understand what was happening," Morimoto said. "He'd have thought that we had sufficient evidence against Mr. Sekikawa. He'd have thought that we had all of the evidence that was needed to conclude the investigation. It must have been quite annoying for him. Still, he couldn't exactly have come over here and asked us what was taking so long, could he!"

Suzuki's face broke into a smile as she considered the amusing prospect of Mr. Ishihara complaining to the police that they were not properly following the clues that he had left them when he murdered Mr. Sekikawa.

"No, sir, he couldn't very well complain to us. It must have been very frustrating for him. And I suppose that after a couple of weeks he realized that his plan hadn't worked, and that the net was still closing in on him. And that's when he decided to end it all and commit suicide."

"And about your second point, sir," Suzuki continued. "About the evidence for it all, the evidence that Mr. Ishihara really did carry out the plan that you outlined, the evidence that our conjecture is correct. Well, actually, as far as I can see, sir, there isn't any real evidence at all. The only evidence we have is that Ms. Sakai told us that Mr. Sekikawa took a telephone call from Mr. Ishihara the night before the murder, and that a rendezvous was arranged for the evening of the murder at Momotaro's statue. That's all the evidence we have, I'm afraid."

Morimoto nodded slowly. He was staring out of the window at the dark sky and thinking.

"However, sir," Suzuki added, "looking at it from the another point of view, there's no evidence that it couldn't have happened according to our conjecture. There's no proof that events didn't unfold in the way that you've just outlined."

CHAPTER 23

▼

The next day, Wednesday, Inspector Morimoto had some other matters to attend to at the beginning of the morning, and it was not until almost midday that he was able to get to police headquarters. When he walked into his office, he was pleased to see that Police Officer Suzuki was at her desk.

Morimoto walked over to the window and looked out. It had not rained for a couple of days, and the rainy season seemed to have come to a close. This meant that they could expect mostly sunshine and high temperatures for a month or so, and that they would be starting the hottest period of the year in Okayama.

Morimoto had come up with some additional ideas concerning the murder case of Mr. Sekikawa, some new ideas that seemed to explain the remaining puzzles in the case. He had been looking forward to being able to discuss them with Suzuki, and he suspected that, as usual, Suzuki had probably hit upon the same solutions to the puzzles that he himself had discovered.

Morimoto sat down at his desk with a cup of tea.

"Suzuki," he began, "about the theory that we discussed yesterday concerning the possibility that Mr. Ishihara planned the murder of Mr. Sekikawa, and that he carried out the murder himself. It still leaves a few important questions that remain unanswered, doesn't it?"

"Yes, sir," Suzuki replied, looking up from her desk, "there are a couple of questions outstanding. I've been thinking about them myself."

"Of course," Morimoto said, "the most curious point of all is the one that Ms. Sakai raised the other day when she came over here to talk to us. She said that she was confused that Mr. Sekikawa had dropped the key off for her. She was quite perplexed about that point. She was quite clear that her arrangement with Mr.

Sekikawa had been that he'd only drop the key off for her if the money was in the locker."

"That's right, sir."

"However, the money wasn't in the locker. It was the computer chip and the documents that were in the locker. Ms. Sakai couldn't understand why Mr. Sekikawa had wanted her to retrieve the chip and the documents from the locker. Their plan was to run away that evening, and what they needed was money."

"Yes, sir, Ms. Sakai did tell us that she found that very difficult to understand. She was obviously very surprised and disappointed when she opened up the umbrella and found the plastic box and the documents instead of the money that she'd been expecting. It seems that Mr. Sekikawa must have thought that the umbrella did have the money concealed inside. Perhaps that's what Mr. Ishihara told him. In any case, he'd have noticed that the umbrella was heavy when he carried it from the hotel to the station, so he must have realized that it had something wrapped inside it."

"And, Suzuki, there are some additional, rather strange aspects about Mr. Ishihara's plan, aren't there? The plan that we've conjectured that Mr. Ishihara made, that is. The most important point, I believe, is the question of why Mr. Ishihara needed a room at the Grandview Hotel at all. We've deduced that he stored the umbrella there, and I think that's what he must have done. But then the question is, why didn't he just put the umbrella in a coin locker by himself?"

"Exactly, sir. I've been wondering about that point myself. It seems that Mr. Ishihara could have put the umbrella in a coin locker at Okayama station by himself on Tuesday night, say. Then when he came back to Okayama on Thursday evening, all that he'd have needed to do would have been to bring the coin locker key with him."

"If he'd wanted to," Suzuki continued, "Mr. Ishihara could have opened up the locker to show Mr. Sekikawa what was inside before they went off, supposedly to meet the syndicates. However, it seems that Mr. Ishihara went to great trouble to take the room at the Grandview Hotel, and it seems that he wanted to take Mr. Sekikawa up to the room in order to get the black umbrella."

"Exactly," Morimoto said. "For some reason, the hotel room at the Grandview Hotel was an essential component of Mr. Ishihara's plan."

Suzuki nodded.

"The problem that Mr. Ishihara was faced with, sir, was that Mr. Sekikawa might want to open the umbrella to check that it had the money inside. It would be disastrous for Mr. Ishihara if Mr. Sekikawa opened the umbrella and found the computer chip and the documents inside. If that happened, then Mr. Ishihara certainly wasn't going to be able to lure Mr. Sekikawa to the alley, and moreover, Mr. Sekikawa would most likely have reported the existence of the chip and the documents to either National Electronics or the police, and Mr. Ishihara would have been discovered as the source of the leaks. Therefore, it's clear that a crucial aspect of Mr. Ishihara's plan must have been to somehow convince Mr. Sekikawa that the black umbrella contained money."

Morimoto and Suzuki looked at each other.

"The questions seem rather difficult to explain at first, don't they Suzuki," Morimoto said quietly, "but I think that there's actually quite a simple explanation, don't you? There's one final aspect of Mr. Ishihara's plan which seems to explain everything, don't you think?"

Suzuki nodded slowly.

"Yes, sir, there is something that would explain it all. I suppose that you're thinking about an umbrella switch, is that right, sir?"

Morimoto grinned, and he swung his legs up onto his desk. He leaned back in his chair and he clasped his hands behind his neck, according to his habit. He himself had also come to the conclusion that there had to have been an umbrella switch.

"Yes, Suzuki," he said triumphantly, "I do believe that you've got it! I really think that you've got it! There was a switch of the umbrella...a switch of the black umbrella!"

In the year and a half that they had been working together, Suzuki had never before seen Morimoto look so happy. In fact, she had never before seen him express as much emotion of any kind as he was displaying at that moment.

"Yes, sir. It would appear so, sir. It would appear that the black umbrella was switched."

"Precisely, and it means that there were actually two switches going on. The keys were switched, and the umbrellas were switched too. Mr. Sekikawa switched the keys, but Mr. Ishihara switched the umbrellas. They were both tricking each other, weren't they?"

"Yes, sir, that would appear to be the simplest explanation."

They sat in silence for a few moments.

"Well, Suzuki," Morimoto began again, "tell me how you think it all happened then."

Suzuki took a deep breath, folded her arms and crossed her legs.

"Well, sir, as you mentioned the other day, what we have to do is to count up all of the umbrellas. We have to keep track of where all of the umbrellas were, and who had them at the various stages of the development of the case. I suppose that it all started out when Mr. Ishihara obtained two identical black umbrellas."

Morimoto nodded.

"And moreover, sir," Suzuki continued, "when Mr. Ishihara checked into the Grandview Hotel on the Tuesday evening, under the false name of Mr. Kuroki, of course, I think that he took both of the black umbrellas up to his room. And he left both of the umbrellas in the room when he left the hotel and went home that evening."

"Also, sir, Mr. Ishihara wrapped the plastic box containing the computer chip and some copies of the sensitive documents from his company inside one of the umbrellas. But the other umbrella was empty—there wasn't anything inside it. And furthermore, Mr. Ishihara must have hidden one of the umbrellas somewhere. He must have made sure that it was completely out of sight. Most probably, he put it in the wardrobe, I suppose. He hid the umbrella that contained the computer chip and the documents. The other black umbrella, the empty one, wouldn't have been hidden. It could have been left anywhere in the room."

"The next development, sir, was on the Thursday night when it was raining heavily. Mr. Sekikawa was waiting at Okayama station next to Momotaro's statue, and he was holding his dark green umbrella. Then Mr. Ishihara arrived on the Nozomi bullet train from Osaka, and he went out to the statue to meet Mr. Sekikawa. According to the account that Ms. Sakai gave us, Mr. Ishihara was using a dark red umbrella at that time."

Suzuki paused for a moment. Morimoto was nodding slowly.

"And then," Suzuki continued, "the two of them walked over to the Grandview Hotel, and they rode the elevator up to room sixteen hundred and three, and they took their umbrellas with them. We'll never know for certain exactly what happened in that hotel room for the three or four minutes that the two of them were in the room together, but we can reasonably imagine a plausible scenario for what might have taken place."

"I believe, sir, that a fundamental element of Mr. Ishihara's scheme was that he wanted to make Mr. Sekikawa think that they were going through with the plan that he'd outlined the evening before during his phone call from Osaka station. In other words, he wanted Mr. Sekikawa to think that he'd brought the money with him from Osaka, and he wanted Mr. Sekikawa to think that they were going to deposit it in the coin locker at Okayama station."

"Therefore, I suppose that Mr. Ishihara must have actually brought the money with him from Osaka. It could perhaps have been the money that Mr. Ishihara had obtained by selling the first computer chip, the money that the Chief told you that he and Mr. Nishi found at Mr. Ishihara's house inside a money belt. So it seems probable, therefore, that Mr. Ishihara came from Osaka on the Nozomi bullet train wearing the money belt that contained all of the money."

"Then, when they were alone in the hotel room, Mr. Ishihara took the money belt off from underneath his shirt, and he showed the money that was inside it to Mr. Sekikawa. Then Mr. Ishihara took the black umbrella that he'd left in the room, the black umbrella that was empty, and they put the money inside the umbrella, and closed it up."

"If this is really what happened, then at this point there'd actually have been four umbrellas in the room. There'd have been Mr. Sekikawa's dark green umbrella and there'd have been Mr. Ishihara's dark red umbrella. Furthermore, there'd also have been the black umbrella that they'd just filled with the money. These are the three umbrellas that Mr. Sekikawa would have been aware of. However, Mr. Ishihara would have known that there was also a fourth umbrella, which was still hidden in the wardrobe. The hidden umbrella was the other black umbrella, which had the computer chip and the company documents wrapped inside it."

"Yes," Morimoto said, "I agree with what you've laid out there. And it must have been at that point that Mr. Ishihara switched the two black umbrellas, don't you think?"

"Exactly, sir. I think that's exactly what happened next. Perhaps Mr. Ishihara asked Mr. Sekikawa to go into the bathroom to get some of the towels wet, or something like that. Anyhow, somehow Mr. Ishihara managed to exchange the two black umbrellas without Mr. Sekikawa noticing. Then, when they left the room and went back down to the lobby in the elevator, we have Ms. Sakai's account that Mr. Ishihara was carrying the dark red umbrella that he'd arrived with, but Mr. Sekikawa was carrying the black umbrella."

"Mr. Sekikawa thought that the black umbrella that he was carrying had the money concealed inside it. After all, he'd just helped Mr. Ishihara hide the money inside a black umbrella. That's why, after they'd put the umbrella in the coin locker, Mr. Sekikawa dropped the key off for Ms. Sakai in the tissue, just as they'd arranged. However, Mr. Ishihara knew that the black umbrella that they'd placed in the coin locker really contained the computer chip and the documents, and that's what Ms. Sakai discovered, much to her chagrin, later that evening in her apartment at Takashima."

Suzuki looked over at Morimoto.

"And that, sir, would seem to explain just about everything. In any case, it provides a resolution for the remaining puzzles that we have with the case. Mr.

Ishihara wanted to frame Mr. Sekikawa by having the missing computer chip and the copies of National Electronics' documents associated with him. So his plan was that he'd murder Mr. Sekikawa, and that we'd find the coin locker key in his pocket, the key to the coin locker at Okayama station where they'd deposited the black umbrella containing the chip and the documents."

Morimoto was nodding.

"Of course, sir," Suzuki continued, "Mr. Ishihara intended that we should find the chip and the documents inside the coin locker. However, Mr. Ishihara wanted Mr. Sekikawa to think that the money was inside the locker, so that's why Mr. Ishihara had to plan some kind of a switch."

"And furthermore, sir, I suppose that's why Mr. Ishihara decided to use the hotel room in the first place, and that's why he decided to use the umbrellas. And moreover, that's why he couldn't have just left the umbrella in the coin locker himself before he went to Osaka. The reason is that he needed to be able to show the money to Mr. Sekikawa, and then he needed to be able to make the switch. Consequently, Mr. Ishihara decided to use the hotel room."

"Yes, that's right, Suzuki. And if that's the case, then Mr. Ishihara must have taken the money with him when he left Okayama on Wednesday morning. I suppose that all of that day while he was at Consolidated Chipboards in Osaka he must have been wearing the money belt under his shirt with the money in it. Similarly, when he left the Crystal House Hotel on the night of the murder to go to the baseball game, he must have been wearing the money belt again."

They sat in silence for a while.

"Well, it's certainly a theory, isn't it?" Morimoto said, eventually. "It's a theory that seems to fit in with all of the facts as we know them, and it's a theory that seems to make sense from the point of view of both Mr. Sekikawa and Mr. Ishihara. It provides a reasonable explanation for how they both acted on that Thursday evening."

"Yes, sir. The entire scenario that we've suggested would, at first sight, seem rather bizarre, rather fantastic. Yet, it does actually provide a fairly simple explanation for the series of events in the murder case that we've observed."

Suzuki's mathematical training from Tokyo University started to reveal itself.

"From a mathematical point of view, sir, the explanation that we've outlined for Mr. Ishihara's activities does seem to provide the simplest solution to all of the questions that have been posed by this case. Even though, on the face of it, our conjecture may appear to be a rather complex solution, nevertheless, we have to remember that the facts that we've been presented with are themselves rather unusual."

"In other words, sir, even though it's a rather convoluted set of events that we're proposing, they have to be considered in the context of the facts of the case that are known to us. In order to solve the case, what we are searching for is the simplest explanation that is consistent with all of the information on the case that we've been able to obtain. And I believe, sir, that the theory we've suggested seems to meet that criterion."

Morimoto stroked his chin.

"Yes," he said, "when solving mysteries like this one, it's always a question of prior probabilities and posterior probabilities. If, two months ago, before any of this had taken place, somebody had outlined to us the plot which we are considering, the plot which involves the switching of coin locker keys, the switching of umbrellas, and the clandestine trips on the Nozomi bullet train with the alibi of the baseball game at the Osaka Dome…if we'd heard that plot described to us, I think that it's fair to say that we'd have been quite incredulous."

"We'd have considered it to be very far-fetched indeed," Morimoto continued. "We'd have thought that it would be very unlikely for such a set of events to actually take place. So, in other words, it is a plot with a very small prior probability. Nevertheless, as we consider the plot in retrospect, as we consider the plot now at the present moment, the situation is quite different."

"The situation is quite different now because of all of the things that have taken place. We are now confronted with a set of observations, or data if you like, which are the deaths of Mr. Sekikawa and Mr. Ishihara, the evidence provided by Ms. Sakai, the coin locker key, the empty coin locker, the umbrella containing the missing computer chip and documents, the results of Mr. Nishi's investigation, and the mysterious Mr. Kuroki who stayed at the Grandview Hotel. So now we have to propose a plot that will explain all of these events which have been observed."

"Consequently, the plot which had a very small prior probability, now seems to be much more reasonable. It seems much more plausible, because it happens to be consistent with what we know about the case. Therefore, its posterior probability can be considered to be quite high. Considered in the light of the facts of the case, as we know them, the plot that we are considering no longer appears to be quite so far-fetched. In fact, as far as I can see, there aren't any other explanations that are quite as plausible as the plot that we've outlined. In other words, nothing else has such a high posterior probability."

"Yes, sir," Suzuki said, "I quite agree with you."

Morimoto and Suzuki thought for a while. Then Suzuki offered some additional comments.

"In any case, sir, the solution that we've suggested does have some rather interesting symmetries to it. It principally involves just two people, Mr. Sekikawa and Mr. Ishihara, who were both independently carrying out switches in an attempt to deceive each other."

"On the one hand, sir, Mr. Sekikawa switched the coin locker keys in an attempt to take the money and run away with Ms. Sakai. On the other hand, Mr. Ishihara switched the umbrellas in an attempt to frame Mr. Sekikawa for the leaks and to save himself. In a way, they both succeeded to some extent, although of course, neither of them completely succeeded."

"As they walked away together from Okayama station for the last time," Suzuki continued, "on the way to the alley where one of them would take the other by surprise and slit his throat, it turns out that neither of them knew exactly what was happening. Mr. Sekikawa thought, incorrectly, that the money was in the coin locker and that Ms. Sakai would be retrieving it for them to run away with. At the same time, Mr. Ishihara thought, again incorrectly, that Mr. Sekikawa was carrying the key to the coin locker with him—the coin locker where they'd just left the umbrella with the incriminating computer chip and documents inside it. Mr. Ishihara thought that he was framing Mr. Sekikawa for the leaking, and that he was thereby removing suspicion from himself. They had both succeeded in tricking each other."

"Yes, and they both eventually ended up dead," Morimoto added.

CHAPTER 24

▼

The final installment of our story takes place two days later on Friday. It was the Friday exactly three weeks after the morning when Inspector Morimoto had been awakened from his sleep by the news that a body had been found in an alley near Okayama station. It was exactly three weeks after Morimoto had stood with his umbrella looking down at the body lying in the rain, and wondering why the dead man had not brought his umbrella with him.

Our final installment, in its own small way, is a victory. It represents a triumph for the art of logical deduction. It pays homage to the accomplishments of those among us who carefully observe and absorb information, who contemplate the meaning of the information, and who search for an explanation that is consistent with what they have found.

Our story provides a reflection on the essence of mankind's scientific reasoning. This is the reasoning that stretches back through the centuries and millennia as we have struggled to comprehend and to make sense of the world in which we live. Our story is a tribute to the scientists, the theoreticians, and the philosophers who have endeavored to understand what they have observed, and who have courageously stepped forward to propose an explanation for life's mysteries.

A good theory is a theory that is the simplest, most straightforward explanation for a set of observations. A very good theory is one that can be validated. A very good theory is a theory from which certain predictions can be inferred, predictions that subsequently can be demonstrated to be true. And this is what will happen to the theory put forward by Inspector Morimoto and Police Officer Suzuki regarding the events on the night of Mr. Sekikawa's murder. We shall see that they will make a prediction from their theory, and that their prediction will be observed to be true.

On that Friday, Morimoto and Suzuki were eating lunch at a restaurant on the second floor of Okayama station. It had been Morimoto's suggestion that they eat there. They had both been in their office all morning working on various other routine matters, and towards the end of the morning Morimoto had suggested that they take lunch together at the station.

It was a very hot day, and they ordered a typical simple summer dish that was delivered to them on large black trays. There was a pile of cold, bright white noodles lying on top of a bamboo mat next to which was a small bowl containing a watery black sauce. They were also given a small raw, spotted quail egg, which they cracked open and added to the sauce. After tipping small piles of thinly sliced onions and grated radish into their sauce bowl, they stirred the mixture with their chopsticks. Then they lifted the noodles off the bamboo mat and into the sauce bowl, one at a time, before eating them.

Morimoto and Suzuki did not talk very much while they were eating, and as a matter of fact, they had not talked about Mr. Sekikawa's murder case at all since Wednesday morning, two days before. When they had finished their cold noodles, Morimoto and Suzuki sipped their cups of hot green tea.

Eventually, Morimoto cleared his throat to speak. He looked up at Suzuki.

"He had to get rid of the umbrellas, didn't he?" Morimoto said rather quietly.

Suzuki nodded. She did not say anything.

"It's not as easy as one would have thought, is it?" Morimoto prompted her. "How do you think that he did it?"

Suzuki sipped her tea before replying.

"Well, sir, from what we know about Mr. Ishihara, he'd have done it very carefully, I believe. They weren't just any umbrellas. One was the umbrella of somebody who he'd just killed, and the other was an exact replica of an umbrella that he thought that we'd found in the coin locker, the umbrella that had the missing computer chip and the documents concealed inside it."

"Those were the items," Suzuki continued, "that Mr. Ishihara thought would have incriminated the dead Mr. Sekikawa as the traitor who'd been responsible for leaking National Electronics' secrets abroad. I think that Mr. Ishihara would have been very careful with those two umbrellas. Very careful indeed."

For the past two days, Morimoto and Suzuki had both been deliberating the final piece of their hypothesis. This was the question of what Mr. Ishihara would have done when he checked out of the hotel on the Saturday morning.

"Mr. Ishihara's problem was that he'd actually have had three umbrellas to deal with that morning," Suzuki explained. "It was raining that Saturday morning, so Mr. Ishihara would naturally have taken his own umbrella with him when he left his house. According to our conjecture, when Mr. Ishihara arrived at the Grandview Hotel he'd have been wearing his disguise. But anyway, he'd still have needed to have an umbrella with him."

"So therefore, sir, when Mr. Ishihara went up to room sixteen hundred and three, there'd actually have been a total of three umbrellas there altogether. In addition to the umbrella that he brought with him that morning, there'd have been the two umbrellas that had been left in the room after his brief visit with Mr. Sekikawa on the Thursday evening. Mr. Sekikawa's dark green umbrella and the black umbrella with the money inside would still have been in the room when he went there on Saturday morning."

"In addition, sir, I expect that Mr. Ishihara also took his empty money belt with him, or maybe he'd just left the empty money belt in the hotel room on Thursday night. In any case, the first thing that he'd have done would have been to take the money out of the black umbrella, and to put it inside the money belt, which he'd presumably have worn underneath his shirt. The money belt and the money would eventually be found back at his house by Mr. Nishi and Special Branch on the night that Mr. Ishihara committed suicide."

"However, sir, the problem that Mr. Ishihara would have faced in the hotel room on Saturday morning was that he'd have had to do something with the dark green umbrella and with the black umbrella. And of course, he wouldn't have wanted to draw any attention to himself, so he surely wouldn't have walked down to the lobby carrying three umbrellas. He wouldn't have wanted to have three umbrellas with him when he walked up to the reception desk to check out, particularly not those umbrellas that were linked to the murder that he'd committed two days before."

Morimoto was nodding.

"And furthermore," Suzuki continued, "Mr. Ishihara wouldn't have wanted to leave the umbrellas in his hotel room after he'd checked out. The hotel might have tried to contact the person who they thought had used the room, which would have been Mr. Kuroki from Tokyo. When the hotel found out that it was a fictitious phone number and address that Mr. Kuroki had used, who knows what they might have done? In any case, sir, it would just have drawn attention to the matter, and I don't think that Mr. Ishihara would have liked that."

"You're right," Morimoto agreed. "According to the theory that we've worked out so far, Mr. Ishihara was a very clever man who thought through each part of his plan very carefully and in meticulous detail. We can therefore reasonably expect that he wouldn't have taken any unnecessary risks with the umbrellas. Nevertheless, he still had to dispose of them somehow."

"That's right, sir. If Mr. Ishihara wasn't going to walk out of the hotel with three umbrellas then he might have decided to just leave the two umbrellas somewhere in the hotel—in one of the public bathrooms, for example. In that case, I expect that they'd have eventually ended up in the hotel lost property. I rather feel, though, that Mr. Ishihara would have preferred to have kept the umbrellas out of sight altogether."

"The thing is though," Suzuki continued, "we also know that Mr. Ishihara didn't have much time that morning. After leaving his house, he'd have gone straight to Okayama station to put on his disguise. Then he wouldn't have had much time before he checked out of the hotel, which we know was at 9:20 that morning."

Morimoto and Suzuki had finished drinking their tea.

"Actually," Morimoto remarked, "I called the manager of the Grandview Hotel this morning. He told me that room sixteen hundred and three isn't being used at the moment. I thought that perhaps we might go over there now and take a look at the room. How about it, Suzuki?"

Now Suzuki understood the real reason why Morimoto had suggested that they take lunch together at Okayama station.

A short while afterwards, Morimoto, Suzuki, and a hotel technician stepped out of the elevator on the sixteenth floor of the Grandview Hotel. They walked along the carpeted hallway in silence, and the only sound was the gentle background music emanating from the small speakers in the ceiling. The technician pulled a key out of his pocket and opened up room sixteen hundred and three.

Morimoto and Suzuki stepped inside the room and looked around. It was very much as they had both expected. It was a very pleasant single hotel room with its own bathroom. There was a bed with a quilt, a chair, and a desk with a large mirror. There was also a wardrobe and a window that overlooked the station below.

When they entered the room, the bathroom door was on their right hand side, and the wardrobe was on their left hand side. In this entrance hallway, the ceiling was quite low. However, the ceiling was much higher in the main part of the room, and on the narrow strip of wall in the room that was over the top of the opening back towards the entrance hallway there was a small metal grill. This ventilation outlet provided the air conditioning and the heating for the room. The temperature controls were on a panel by the side of the bed.

Morimoto looked up at the grill.

"Excuse me," he said to the technician. "Is it very difficult to remove that grill?"

"Not at all, Inspector, as long as you have a screwdriver with you," the technician replied.

"Well, then, could you take it off, please?"

"Very well, sir."

The technician moved the chair over from the desk and placed it underneath the grill. He removed his shoes and climbed up onto the chair. He then pulled out a screwdriver from his overalls. The grill was rectangular in shape and it had six small screws that needed removing, one from each corner and one from the middle of each of the two longer sides. As he removed the screws the technician placed them inside his top pocket, one by one. Finally, he was able to pull the grill off the wall, and he stepped down from the chair and laid it on the carpet.

"Just a moment, sir," the technician exclaimed in an astonished voice. "I think that I saw something inside."

The technician climbed back up onto the chair and put his hand inside the hole in the wall. He seemed quite surprised to find two rather dusty objects inside the ventilation shaft. He took them out and handed them down to Morimoto. One was a dark green umbrella and the other was a black umbrella.

Suzuki sat down on the edge of the bed. She started smiling, and then she started to laugh gently as she looked over at Inspector Morimoto and the two umbrellas.

0-595-30979-8

CPSIA information can be obtained at www.ICGtesting.com
Printed in the USA
LVOW071921120911

245973LV00001B/46/A